THE MYSTERY OF THE ENCHANTED CRYPT

Also by Eduardo Mendoza at Telegram

No Word from Gurb

Eduardo Mendoza

The Mystery
of the Enchanted Crypt

Translated from the Spanish by
Nick Caistor

TELEGRAM
London San Francisco Beirut

First published as *El Misterio de la Cripta Embrujada*
by Seix Barral, Barcelona, 1979
This English translation published in 2008 by Telegram

ISBN: 978-1-84659-051-1

Manufactured in Lebanon

TELEGRAM
26 Westbourne Grove, London W2 5RH
825 Page Street, Suite 203, Berkeley, California 94710
Tabet Building, Mneimneh Street, Hamra, Beirut
www.telegrambooks.com

CONTENTS

I

A SURPRISE VISIT

Victory was ours for the taking. I'm not one to boast, but the tactics I had devised, plus the rigorous training I put the lads through, as well as the hope and fear of God I instilled in them, all gave us the edge. Everything was going as planned: we seemed bound to score, the opposing team was on the point of collapse. It was a beautiful April morning, and out of the corner of my eye I could see the mulberries growing round the pitch were covered in a fluffy yellow down that offered the first scent of spring. But then everything started to go wrong: the sky suddenly clouded over, and Carrascosa from Ward 13, whom I had told to defend stoutly and, if necessary, illegally, threw himself to the ground and began to scream that he didn't want to see his hands dripping with human blood, which nobody had asked him to do, and that his mother was watching from on high and was taking him to task for his murderous tackles. It was no excuse, she said, that he was merely following orders. Fortunately, I combined my role as centre-forward with that of referee, so I was able, despite loud protests, to annul the goal our opponents had just scored against us. I knew though that, once things began to go wrong, it could only get worse, and that our sporting fate was hanging by a thread. When I saw Toñito head-butting the opposition goalposts whenever he made a mess of one of the long and (why deny it) accurate through-balls I sent him from mid-field, I realised the game was up, and that we weren't going to be champions this year either. That was why I didn't mind so much when Dr Chulferga (if that really was his name, because I've never seen it written and I'm rather hard of hearing) gesticulated for me to leave the field and join him on the far side of the touchline. He said he had something to tell me. Dr Chulferga was a young, stockily built man with a beard as thick as his brown-tinted glasses. He had recently arrived from South America, and nobody liked him much. In order to conceal my confusion, I bowed my head in greeting.

'Dr Sugrañes wants to see you,' he said.

To keep the conversation going, I replied: 'It will be my pleasure.' When this did not raise a smile, I quickly added: 'Despite the fact that exercise is an excellent tonic for our troubled souls.'

At this, the doctor turned on his heel and strode away, looking back occasionally to make sure I was following him. Ever since that article of his, he had become suspicious. The article, 'Split Personality, Libidinous Fantasies and Urine Retention', had been published by a pro-Franco magazine (taking advantage of the fact of his recent arrival in Spain) as 'Portrait of the Monarchic Personality', with his name prominently displayed. Dr Chulferga had never got over it: in the middle of a therapy session he was known to exclaim:

'In this shite-house of a country even the lunatics are fascist.'

All of which, as I was saying, led me to follow his orders without a word of protest, although I would have liked to ask permission to have a shower and change my clothes. The fact is I had sweated quite a lot, and I have tendency to BO, especially in closed-in spaces. But I said nothing.

We walked back up the gravel path lined with lime trees, climbed the marble front steps and found ourselves inside the entrance hall of the asylum building, or asylum for short. A pale amber light shone through the glass dome of the hall, seeming to preserve the chill of the last days of winter. At the far end, to the right of the statue of Saint Vincent de Paul, between the pedestal and the carpeted staircase (the one for visitors) stood Dr Sugrañes' waiting-room. As usual, the only things of interest in the room were a few back issues of the Automobile Club magazine gathering dust on the table, but in the far wall stood the solid mahogany door that led to the doctor's consulting room. My companion knocked on it. A green light flashed in a tiny set of traffic lights set in the door-frame. Dr Chulferga opened the door a few inches, stuck his head inside, and muttered a few words. He then pulled his head back on to his shoulders, swung the heavy door open wide, and signalled for me to go in. I was slightly reluctant to do so because it was not often, apart from my three-monthly interview (and that was still five weeks away) that Dr Sugrañes asked to see me, and when he did it was invariably bad news. Perhaps it was this confusion which meant that, although usually I am quite observant, this time I failed to see that apart from the doctor himself there were two other people in the room.

'May I, Doctor?' I said, my voice sounding slightly shrill and uncertain.

'Yes, yes, come in, don't be afraid,' he replied, interpreting my hesitation with his usual perspicacity. 'As you can see, there are some people here to see you.'

At this, I had to stare hard at a diploma hanging on the wall to conceal the way my teeth had begun to chatter.

'Aren't you going to say hello to these kind persons?' said Dr Sugrañes in what sounded to me like a gentle ultimatum.

I made a great effort to collect my thoughts: the first thing to do was to find out who these visitors were, because otherwise I could not guess the purpose of their visit and make sure it had nothing to do with me. To do this I would have to look them in the face, since I deduced this would be the only way of finding out who they were: I had no friends, and in all the five years I had been in the asylum had never received a single visit, since I no longer saw anything of my closest relatives, and with good reason. I therefore began to look round the room as slowly and carefully as possible, hoping nobody would notice. I failed completely in this, as Dr Sugrañes and the other two had all their six eyes trained on me. I will however describe what I saw: in the two leather armchairs opposite Dr Sugrañes' desk (or rather, what had been leather armchairs until Jaimito Bullón forgot himself on one of them, which meant that for reasons of symmetry both of them had to be re-upholstered in purple machine-washable imitation suede) sat the same number of persons. I will now proceed to describe one of them: in the armchair near the window – near that is in relation to the other one, since between the first armchair (the one near the window) and the second there was enough room to place an ashtray on a stand, a very pretty glass ashtray which stood proudly atop a three-foot high bronze column (and I say 'stood' advisedly, because ever since Rebolledo tried to smash the stand over Dr Sugrañes' head, both of them, stand and ashtray, had been removed and nothing put in their place) – anyway, as I was saying, in that chair sat a woman of uncertain age, which I put at around a care-worn fifty. Despite the fact that she seemed to be dressed from charity shops, her manner and features looked distinguished. On the lap of her pleated tergal skirt she was holding a battered, oblong medical bag with a length of rope for a handle. She was smiling through closed lips. Her gaze was penetrating, and her thick eyebrows were furrowed, which caused a horizontal crease to spread across her brow. Apart from this, her forehead was as smooth as the rest of her skin, which showed no signs of make-up, but did show the hint of a moustache. From all the aforementioned I deduced I was in the presence of a nun, a conclusion which, coming as it did from me, was not without merit, since when I was locked up it was not common (although I believe it has since become so) for nuns to go about not wearing habits, at least outside their convent walls. I must admit to being pointed in the right direction by the fact that this lady was wearing a small crucifix on her chest, had a religious medallion hanging round her neck, and carried a heavy rosary tucked into her waistband. Now I will describe the other person, or, if you prefer, the person sitting in the other chair, the one nearer the door that led into the room, if you came the same way as I did. As I was saying, this was a man of roughly the same age as the nun and even, I thought to myself, the same as that of Dr Sugrañes, although I quickly rejected the idea that there was some link between the two. This man's somewhat coarse features were entirely unremarkable apart from the fact that they were well known to me, coinciding, or to be more conceptually accurate, belonging to those of Inspector Flores of the Criminal Investigation Department; in fact, I should say they were Inspector Flores, since it is hard to imagine an inspector without his own facial characteristics or mutatis mutando, any other human being either. I noticed that despite all the lotions and poultices he had used over the years he was now completely bald, so I said:

'Inspector Flores, for you time has stood still.'

To which the inspector made no reply, merely waving a hand as if to say:

'How's it going?'

On top of all this, Dr Sugrañes then pressed a button on the intercom on his desk and said to the voice that came crackling through:

'Pepita, bring a Pepsi-Cola, would you?'

This must surely be for me, I thought, and smiled as pleasantly as I could, although my naturally shy nature may have turned the expression into something of a grimace. Without further ado, I will now proceed to describe the conversation that took place there, in that office.

'I dare say you remember Inspector Flores here,' said Dr Sugrañes, addressing me. 'He was the one who used to arrest, question, and occasionally rough you up whenever your, ahem ... psychic disorder led you to commit anti-social acts.' I nodded. 'None of which, as you well know, was done with any kind of ill-feeling, proof of which, as you have both assured me, is the fact that the two of you have occasionally worked together, that is to say that you unselfishly have offered him your services, which I take as further proof of the ambivalence of your former attitude.'

At this I nodded a second time, since it was true that in my more desperate moments I had stooped low enough to become a police informer in return for a fleeting indulgence on their part, conduct which had never failed to stir animosity among my colleagues who lived outside the law as it now stands, and which had in the long run done me more harm than good.

As befits someone who has scaled the ladder and reached a pre-eminent position in his chosen field, the convoluted but sybilline Dr Sugrañes said nothing further to me, but then turned (orally, at least) to Inspector Flores, who was listening to this man of science with a dead cigar between his lips, eyes half-closed as though he were pondering on its virtues – those of the cigar, I mean.

'Inspector,' said the doctor, pointing to me but talking to the inspector, 'You see before you a new man, someone from whom we have banished all traces of insanity, an achievement for which we medical experts cannot claim all the credit, since as you well know, in our line of work a cure depends almost entirely on the subject's will, and in the case which concerns us, I am delighted to say that the patient ...' – at this he pointed to me again, as if there might be more than one patient in the room, 'has made such a great effort that I would describe his conduct as being the opposite of criminal, that is to say exemplary.'

'Why then,' the nun opened her mouth to say, 'why, Doctor, if I may be allowed to ask a question which you as an expert on the subject might consider superfluous, why then is this, ahem, individual still kept in here?'

She had a metallic, slightly hoarse voice. I could see the words emerging from her mouth like bubbles, where the speech was merely the outer coating which, as the sound burst forth, revealed its ethereal volume: their meaning. Dr Sugrañes prepared to explain at length:

'Well now, the case in question is somewhat complex, straddling as it does two competing authorities. This, ahem, ahem, person was placed in my care by the judicial authorities, who in their wisdom declared that he was more suitable for treatment in a centre such as ours than in a penal institution. In consequence, a decision about his freedom is not my sole responsibility. As you may know, it is an open secret that, whether for ideological or professional reasons, between the magistrature and the medical profession, there is little common ground. I trust that this commentary will not go beyond these walls.' At this he smiled like a man long accustomed to dealing with delicate matters of this kind. 'If it had been up to me, I would have signed his release papers long ago. Similarly, if this, ahem, subject had not been kept in an asylum for all these years, he would by now be out of jail on parole. But things being as they are, I only have to suggest something for the relevant judicial board to rule the opposite. What can you do?'

What Dr Sugrañes was saying was true: I myself had on several occasions asked to be set free, but had always come up against insoluble jurisdictional conflicts. For the past year and a half I had been filling in forms and stealing certificates from the local post office to prove my sanity, only to have everything returned stamped in red with the message 'Does not apply!' and nothing else.

'However,' continued the doctor after a brief pause, 'it seems to me that the circumstances which have brought you, Inspector, and you, Reverend Mother, to my office, could perhaps help break the vicious circle in which we seem to be trapped.'

From their respective chairs, the two visitors voiced their agreement.

'That is to say,' said the doctor, 'if I were to certify that from a medical point of view, the condition of the, ahem, ahem, person in question is favourable, and you, Inspector, were to give, shall we say, your administrative seal of approval to my judgment, and you, Reverend Mother, were to tactfully drop a respectful hint in the archbishop's palace, perhaps the judicial authorities could see their way to ...'

Fine.

I think the moment has come to clear up any lingering doubts kind readers may harbour about me: I am, or rather used to be (and not alternately but concurrently), a lunatic, rogue, criminal and a person almost totally lacking any education or culture. The street was my only school; my only teachers the shameless louts I mixed with. Yet I was never, and still am not, slow on the uptake: fine words, especially when strung on the bracelet of correct syntax, may dazzle me for a moment, throw me off balance, or blur my vision of reality, but this never lasts – my instinct for survival is too well-developed, my fondness for life too deep-seated, my experience of this kind of thing too bitter. Sooner or later, the light comes on in my brain and I understand, as I did on this occasion, that the conversation I am part of had been previously orchestrated and rehearsed, with no other aim than to convince me of some idea or other. But what idea? That I was to spend the rest of my days in the asylum?

'... to show, in short, that the, ahem, ahem, individual we have before us is, not a reformed or rehabilitated character, because that would be to presume his guilt,' – Dr Sugrañes was addressing me again, so I was sorry to have been so caught up in my thoughts that I had missed the first two lines of his speech – 'and which I therefore categorically reject.' The psychiatrist in him was speaking: 'But rather, someone who is reconciled to himself and to society, in a state of reciprocal harmony. Have I made myself clear? Oh good, here's the Pepsi-Cola.'

In normal circumstances I would have thrown myself on the nurse, and while with one hand I tried to fondle the soft, juicy pair of melons straining against the starched white front of her uniform, with the other I'd have snatched the Pepsi-Cola and guzzled it down straight from the bottle, and then perhaps even belched to show my satisfaction. But on this occasion I did nothing of the sort.

I did nothing of the sort because I realised that within these four walls (the ones that made up Dr Sugrañes' office) something very important to me was being hatched, and that if it was to turn out to my advantage it was essential for me to show restraint. I therefore waited while the nurse (trying desperately to drive from my mind the image I had of her from peering through the staff toilet keyhole) filled a cardboard cup with the brown, bubbling liquid and held it out to me as though to say 'drink me'. I took great care to position my lips one on either side of the rim, and not both on the inside, which is my usual way of drinking, and to take sips, rather than noisily slurping it down. I also made sure not to get over-excited and to keep my arms close by my sides so as to keep the sour smell from my armpits from invading the room. I sipped my drink for some length of time, in perfect control of myself, which meant I could not concentrate on what was being said around me. In the end, however, despite the delightful giddy feeling the delicious liquid produced, I did pay attention, and this was what I heard:

'So, do we all agree?'

'As far as I'm concerned,' said Inspector Flores, 'I have no real objection, provided that this, ahem, ahem, person is in agreement.'

I immediately gave my unconditional assent, even though I

was not sure what I was agreeing to. I was old enough to know that anything decided by the three greatest powers on earth, namely justice, science and religion, while not necessarily being for my good, was at the same time beyond objection.

'Considering therefore that this, ahem, ahem, personage,' said Dr Sugrañes, 'gives his full consent, I will leave you to fill him in on the details. And since I am sure you will not want to be disturbed, allow me to demonstrate how this ingenious set of traffic lights I have had installed in the door works. By pressing this red button here, the same colour light flashes outside, signifying that under no circumstances is the person inside the room to be disturbed. The green light signals the exact opposite, while the amber one – as described in the Highway Code, although I would simply call it yellow – means that the occupier, while preferring a discreet privacy, is not averse to being warned in cases of dire emergency – the judgement of which is left to the operator of said invention. Since this is the first time you are using the apparatus, might I suggest you use only the red and green buttons? If you need any clarification, do not hesitate to call me or the nurse, who is still standing here holding an empty, non-returnable bottle.'

Saying this, but not before standing up and covering the distance between his chair and the door, he opened the latter and left, together with the nurse Pepita. It was my suspicion that their relation went far beyond the strictly professional, although I had never managed to catch them in flagrante, despite spending hours watching them come and go, and sending several anonymous letters to the doctor's wife in the hope of making them so nervous they would slip up.

In the situation in which I found myself, and rather than do what any normal person would have done in my shoes, in other words play with the traffic lights, I did not even suggest the idea but, as proof of my perspicacity, let Inspector Flores press whichever button he chose. After so doing, he returned to his chair and said:

'I don't know if you remember,' – by you, he meant me – 'the strange case that happened six years ago now in the San Gervasio school run by the Lazarist nuns. Try to remember.'

I did not have to try hard, because the case had left a significant gap in my memory, or more precisely a gap in my mouth where none other than Inspector Flores had popped out a tooth, convinced as he seemed to be that with a tooth missing I was sure to provide him with the information which to my great regret I did not possess – because if I had known what he was talking about I would still be in possession of a tooth which I have had to do without ever since, since orthodontics has always been beyond my means. In spite of this, and since my knowledge of the affair had in fact been slight, I begged him to tell me all the details, and promised him my full co-operation. As I said this, I kept my mouth tight shut, in case the sight of the gap in my teeth gave him an urge to repeat the procedure. The inspector asked the nun, who was still sitting there, for permission to relight his cigar in order to smoke. Permission having been granted, he proceeded to do so, lying back in his armchair, blowing smoke rings from his mouth and nose, and launching into what in essence comprises the second chapter of my story.

2

THE INSPECTOR'S STORY

'As you are doubtless unaware, the school run by the Lazarist nuns,' began the inspector, studying his cigar as though contemplating how all the money he had paid for it was going up in smoke, 'is situated on a quiet, steep, side street typical of those that wind their way round the aristocratic neighbourhood of San Gervasio, which these days has rather come down in the world. The school prides itself on taking children from only the best Barcelona families, from whom it makes a considerable profit. Please correct me if I say anything out of turn, Reverend Mother. Obviously, the school is for girls only, and has boarding facilities. To complete the picture, I should say that all the pupils wear grey uniforms expressly designed to conceal their burgeoning forms. The school is enveloped in a halo of unassailable worthiness. Are you following me so far?'

Although I had my doubts, I said I was, because I was anxious to get to the dirty bits which I was sure would follow, although I should be honest right away and admit they never did.

'Well then,' continued Inspector Flores, 'on the morning of the seventh of April six years ago, that is in 1971, the person in charge of ensuring that all the girls had woken up, done their ablutions, combed their hair and were dressed and ready for early morning mass, realised that one of them was missing. When the lady asked her classmates, no one knew anything about her disappearance. She went to the dormitory, and found the girl's bed empty. She inspected the bathroom and elsewhere. She searched high and low in the remotest corners of the school. All to no avail. One of the pupils had vanished without trace. All that was missing from her personal effects were the clothes she had been wearing – that is, a nightdress. On her bedside table were found her wristwatch, a pair of cultivated pearl earrings, and the pocket money the disappeared girl had been given to purchase treats in the tuck-shop run by the nuns. Dismayed at what had happened, the person in question told the Mother Superior, and the Reverend Mother imparted the information to the rest of the religious community. A second search was carried out, which proved equally fruitless. At approximately ten in the morning, the girl's parents were informed, and following a brief discussion the affair was put in the police's hands, personified by those you see in front of you now, the very ones which smashed your teeth in.'

'With the alacrity that characterised the forces of order in the pre-post Franco era, I made my way to the school, questioned all those I judged it necessary to question, and then returned to Headquarters. I had the usual police informers brought in, amongst whom you were lucky enough to count yourself, you miserable stool-pigeon, and I subtly extracted from them and you all they knew. By nightfall, however, I had come to the conclusion that the case was a complete mystery. How could a young girl get up in the middle of the night and force the lock on the dormitory door without waking any of her companions? How could she have got through the locked doors separating the dormitory from the garden – that is, if my calculations are correct, at least four or five, depending on whether you go through the toilets on the first floor or not? How could she have walked across the garden in the dark without leaving a single footprint, crushing any flowers or, even more oddly, without revealing her presence to the two mastiffs let loose each night once last prayers have been said? How was she able to climb over the four-metre high spiked railings, or the garden walls of similar height, topped with shards of glass and rolls of barbed wire?'

'How indeed?' I asked, scarcely able to contain my curiosity.

'It's a mystery,' replied the inspector, flicking the ash from his cigar onto the carpet – as I explained, the ashtray and its bronze stand had long ago been removed, and Dr Sugrañes did not smoke. 'But that wasn't the end of the matter, or I wouldn't be here now giving such a lengthy introduction.'

'My investigation had only just begun, but seemed to be heading nowhere, when I received a phone call from the Mother Superior of the school. She, by the way, was not the one you see here,' he jerked his thumb towards the nun, 'but another, rather older one, who with all due respect was not the brightest spark. She begged me to return to the school because she needed to talk to me urgently. I don't believe I've explained, but this occurred on the morning after the girl's disappearance: is that clear? Good. Well, as I was saying, I jumped into a patrol car and thanks to our siren and my waving a threatening fist out of the window the whole time, we managed to get from Via Layetana down in the port up to San Gervasio in less than half an hour, even though the traffic was solid all along Diagonal Avenue.'

'When I was shown into the Mother Superior's office she was accompanied by a man and a woman of well-mannered, wealthy appearance, who identified themselves as the father and mother of the victim. They then immediately, in virtue of the powers that their position conferred on them, ordered me to drop any further investigation into the case – an order with which the Mother Superior concurred in the most emphatic way, even though nobody had asked her opinion. Since it occurred to me that the girl's kidnappers might have warned her parents (thanks to goodness knows what terrible threats) to behave in this way, and since I also knew that the aforementioned attitude is to be discouraged at all costs, I advised them to change their minds. 'You stick to your affairs,' the girl's father told me in so high-handed a tone I can only think he must have been related to His Excellence, 'and I'll take care of mine.'

'If you follow this course of action,' I warned him as I retreated towards the door, 'you will never see your sweet little girl again.'

'The sweet little girl,' said the father clinchingly, 'has

already been recovered. You can go about your business.'
Which is precisely what I did.

'May I ask a question, Inspector?' I said.

'That depends,' he replied, screwing up his face.

'How old was the aforementioned sweet little girl when she disappeared?'

Inspector Flores stared at the nun, who raised her eyebrows in response. The inspector cleared his throat and said:

'Fourteen.'

'Thank you, Inspector. Please be so kind as to continue.'

'For clarity's sake,' said the inspector, 'I think it would be better if the Mother Superior here continues the story.'

At this the nun leapt in so eagerly I thought she must have been dying to get a word in for some time now.

'As far as I have been able to gather,' she began, 'because I have no direct knowledge of these events – they took place at a time when I was in charge of a retreat in the province of Albacete for nuns who were either too old or too young – the decision to cut short the investigation when it had barely begun, to abort it, you might say (were that term not so surrounded by all kinds of polemical connotations), was taken by the missing girl's parents. At first, the then Mother Superior – a very talented and strong-minded woman, may I say in passing – was completely opposed to the idea. She was concerned of course not only about the fate of the girl, but the reputation of the school as a whole. Her protests fell on deaf ears: the parents insisted it was their right as legal guardians of the child, and even mentioned the contributions they made each year to the school for its Christmas of the Poor, Clothing Aid Fortnight, and Founder's Day – which, I might add, is next week.'

'Keeping her reservations to herself therefore, the Mother Superior agreed to their demand, and encouraged the school community and the other pupils to say absolutely nothing about what had happened.'

'Forgive me for interrupting, Reverend Mother,' I ventured to say, 'but there's one point I should like clarified: had the girl really reappeared or not?'

The nun was about to reply when the sound of bells led her to realise what time of day it was.

'It's noon,' she said. 'Would you mind if I collected my thoughts for a few moments to say the Angelus?'

Of course not, we answered in unison.

'Would you be so kind as to put out your cigar?' the nun asked the inspector.

She bowed her head and murmured some prayers. After which she said:

'You may light your cigar again. What was it you asked me?'

'If the girl had reappeared.'

'Ah yes,' she replied, 'after on the previous evening everyone at the school had prayed to our Virgin of the Carmen for a miracle – by the way, I have a supply of blessed medallions of her in my bag, should you wish to purchase any – on the morning of the second day, to their immense surprise the girls discovered that their vanished companion was back in her own bed. She got up with the rest of the girls and performed her daily ablutions along with them, then joined the line-up outside the chapel as if nothing unusual had happened. Faithfully following their instructions, her companions said not a word about it, but this was not the case of the person responsible for making sure that all the girls had got up, done their ablutions, combed their hair, put on their uniforms and were ready to attend the holy mass – the matron, as the person carrying out the aforementioned duties is often known. She, taking the girl by the hand, or possibly by the ear, ran to the Mother Superior – that wonderful person – who could not believe her eyes or ears either. The Reverend Mother wished of course to hear first hand from the girl what had happened, but found that she could not answer any of her questions. She had no idea what they were talking about. Years of experience in dealing with young girls and a profound awareness of human nature led the Mother Superior to realise that the girl was not lying, and that this must be a case of partial amnesia. There was nothing for it but to call the girl's parents and inform them of what had happened. They came speedily to the school and held a lengthy, difficult and secret conversation with her, the upshot of which was that they were determined, as you have heard, that the investigation should be closed, although they never explained the reasons for their decision. The Mother Superior respected their wishes, but observed that in view of what had gone on she would have to ask the parents to take the girl back into their charge, as there was no way she could allow her to stay on at the school. She gave them the name of a non-religious academy where we often send girls who cannot keep up or are too rebellious. And that was the end of the case of the disappeared girl.'

At this, the nun stopped speaking, and silence fell on Dr Sugrañes' office. I wondered if that was all. I could not see the point of these two eminent people, overwhelmed as they must have been with the weight of their respective responsibilities, wasting so much time and saliva over telling me a story like this. I wanted to encourage them to continue, but all I succeeded in doing was crossing my eyes in the most horrible way imaginable. The Mother Superior stifled a cry, while the inspector threw the remains of his cigar out of the window in a perfect arc. There was a further embarrassed silence, until all of a sudden the cigar came flying back in through the window, thrown no doubt by one of the inmates, who must have thought this was some kind of test which could lead to his release if he got it right.

Once the cigar episode had drawn to a close, the inspector and the Reverend Mother exchanged knowing glances, and the former said something so quietly I could not grasp it. I begged him to repeat what he had said, and he complied, the following being a rough approximation of his words:

'It's happened again.'

'What's happened again?' I asked.

'Another girl has disappeared.'

'Another one, or the same one?'

'Another one, you idiot,' the inspector exploded. 'Didn't you hear that the first one was expelled?'

'When did this happen?'

'Last night.'

'What were the circumstances?'

'The same as before, except that everyone involved was different: the vanished girl, her companions, the matron, if that is what she is called, and the former Mother Superior, about whom I reiterate my unfavourable opinion.'

'What about the girl's parents?'

'And the girl's parents, obviously.'

'Not so obviously. It could have been the previous girl's sister.'

The inspector took this blow to his pride on the chin.

'It could have been, but it isn't,' was all he said. 'But it would be useless to deny that the affair – because we may well be facing two episodes of the same event – or the affairs, if there turn out to be two of them, has or have created something of a stink. It also goes without saying that both myself and the Reverend Mother here are anxious for the aforementioned affair or affairs to be successfully resolved as quickly as possible, without involving either of the institutions we represent in any kind of scandal. In order to achieve this, we need someone with a thorough knowledge of the less salubrious sectors of our society, someone whose name can be dragged through the mud without any of it sticking to us, someone who can do our dirty work but who if need be we can deny all knowledge of. You will not be surprised to hear that you are that someone. Mention has already been made of how a discreet and efficient collaboration in this affair or affairs might be of advantage to you, while I leave it to you to imagine what the consequences of an accidental or intentional slip-up could be. On no account are you to go anywhere near the school or the disappeared girl's relatives – nor do we have any intention of telling you her name. You are immediately to inform me, and only me, of anything you discover; you are to take no initiatives not suggested or ordered by me, depending on the mood I'm in, and you will pay for any deviation from these instructions with my anger and the usual way I have of relieving it. I hope I have made myself clear.'

Since this ominous threat, which required no response on my part, appeared to be the culmination of our little chat, the inspector pressed the traffic light button once more, and Dr Sugrañes appeared soon afterwards. I could not help thinking he had taken advantage of his absence from the room to give the nurse one.

'It's all settled, Doctor,' the inspector announced. 'We'll take this, ahem, ahem, pearl with us, and we'll inform you in due course of our most interesting psychopathic experiment. Many thanks for your invaluable help, and good luck to you. Hey you, are you deaf?' It goes without saying that these last words were aimed at me rather than Dr Sugrañes. 'Can't you see we're leaving?'

With that they set off, not even giving me time to gather up my few possessions. This was no great loss, but I did regret not being able to take a shower, as this meant that the stink from my armpits soon filled the interior of the police patrol car in which, thanks to the frequent use of horn, siren and some smart manoeuvring, we were conveyed in less than an hour to the centre of Barcelona and by the same token to the end of this second chapter.

3

A RE-ENCOUNTER,
AN ENCOUNTER AND A JOURNEY

As I sat dazzled by the lively bustle of a Barcelona I had not seen in five years, I was helped out of the car by a well-aimed kick to the rear, just as we were passing the Canaletas fountain. I quickly and gratefully drank a few mouthfuls of its chlorinated water. I must make a small, personal parenthesis here to say that my initial sensation on finding myself free and able to do as I pleased was one of great joy. After this parenthesis, I feel obliged to add that I was immediately assailed by all kinds of doubts. I had no friends, money or place to live, and had only the clothes I was standing up in, to whit a filthy, worn hospital gown. And yet I had been charged with a mission I suspected would be full of dangers and difficulties.

I decided my first move should be to find something to eat. It was mid-afternoon and I hadn't had a bite since breakfast. I searched through the waste bins in the square around me, and it was not long before I came across half a bread roll, or hot-dog as I believe they are called, which some satisfied customer must have thrown away. Despite its somewhat acid taste and cotton wool consistency, I made short work of it. Replenished, I wandered down the Ramblas, admiring the trade in cheap goods taking place all along the pavements, and waiting for night to fall. I knew this could not be long in coming, because the light was already fading.

The merry vice dens of the Barrio Chino were in full swing by the time I reached my goal – a dive called Leash's American Bar, Leeches for short, located in a basement on the corner of Calle Robador. This was where I was hoping to make my first and most reliable contact, and so it proved, because no sooner had I entered the doorway and my eyes become accustomed to the gloom, than at a nearby table I spied the blonde curls and greenish skin of a woman who, since she was sitting with her back to the door, did not see me come in, but went on cleaning her ears with one of those flat toothpicks bus conductors and other minor officials like to chew. When I finally appeared in her line of vision, she opened her stuck-on eyelashes as far as her skin would permit, while at the same time dropping her jaw so far I could see her mouthful of rotten teeth.

'Hello there, Candida,' I said, this being the name of my sister, who was the person now before me, 'it's been a while.' As I spoke, I had to force a painful smile, because seeing the ravages that time and life had wreaked on her face brought tears of pity to my eyes. When she was a teenager, someone, heaven knows why, had told my sister she looked like Judy Garland. She had believed them, poor girl, and still clung to the illusion thirty years later. Nothing could have been further from the truth: if my memory serves me right, Judy Garland was a good-looking, cheerful woman, neither of which attributes, I would say as a neutral observer, were characteristics my sister was blessed with. On the contrary, she had a bulbous, pitted forehead, tiny eyes that tended to cross when she was worried about something, a snub, piggy nose, a mouth that drooped to one side, and uneven, yellow buck teeth. The less said about her body the better. She had never recovered from birth, a birth that had brought her into the world in a hasty, cack-handed way, in the back room of the ironmonger's where my mother had desperately tried to abort her, with the result that her body had come out like a bag of nails, far too large for her short, bowed legs. This gave her the look of an overgrown dwarf, a description used by the photographer (in that heartless way artists have) when he refused to take her picture on the day of her first communion, complaining she would crack his lens.

'You're looking younger and prettier than ever.'

'Holy shit! You've escaped from the asylum!' was her response.

'That's where you're wrong, Candida: they've let me out. Can I sit down?'

'No.'

'As I was saying, I was let out this afternoon, and I said to myself, what's the very first thing you want to do, what would be your heart's desire?'

'I promised Santa Rosa a candle if they kept you inside for life,' she said with a sigh. 'Have you eaten? If not, ask them for a roll at the bar, and tell them to put it on my slate. But I swear I'm not going to give you a cent.'

In spite of her apparent harshness, I knew my sister cared for me. I suspect that for her I was the child she could never have, because whether as a result of a congenital defect, or due to the harsh life she had known, her maternal instincts had been thwarted by the fact that her insides were full of holes, so that her uterus, spleen and colon were in direct contact with each other – which turned any internal process into an unpredictable and cataclysmic event.

'I would never dream of asking you, Candida.'

'You look a real mess.'

'I didn't manage to have a shower after the match.'

'I wasn't only talking about your smell.' She paused for a minute, which I thought must mean she was reflecting on how the years roll by, devouring our fleeting youth in their merciless maw. 'But before you make yourself scarce, clear one thing up for me, will you: if it's not money you're after, what are you doing here?'

'Above all, to see how you are getting along. And once I had reassured myself that things couldn't be better, to ask you the smallest of favours, so tiny it hardly counts as one at all.'

'Shove off,' she said, waving a stubby hand stained by nicotine and cheap jewellery.

'Just some information that will cost you nothing but which could mean a lot to me. Not so much information as a bit of gossip, an inoffensive rumour you might have heard ...'

'You aren't back with that Inspector Flores, are you?'

'No, my love, why do you say that? Just idle curiosity on my part, that's all. That girl ... the one from the school in San Gervasio ...what was her name? It was in the papers ... the one who disappeared a couple of days ago. Do you know who I'm talking about?'

'I don't know a thing. And even if I did, I wouldn't tell you. It's a murky business. How far is Flores involved?'

'Up to here,' I said, patting the top of my abundant crop of hair, where now, alas! the first silver threads were starting to appear.

'Then it's even murkier than I thought. What's your interest?'

'My freedom.'

'Go back to the asylum: you've got bed, board and three meals a day there. What more d'you want?' The thick coating of make-up could not conceal her concern.

'I want to try my luck outside.'

'I couldn't give a damn what happens to you, so long as you don't drag me into it. And don't try to tell me that this time it'll be different, because ever since you were born you've done nothing but cause me problems. I'm too old for that sort of thing. Go on, get out of here. I'm waiting for a client.'

'With those good looks of yours, they must be queuing up,' I said, knowing my sister was very susceptible to praise, perhaps because life had not exactly been kind to her. When she was nine she was considered so ugly she wasn't allowed to sing 'Somewhere Over the Rainbow', after six months of exhausting attempts to learn it, on a charity show organised by Radio Nacional. At such a tender age, these things leave a scar for life, especially as she had contributed a not inconsiderable sum to their good works, collected by selling her pachydermic backside to the old, half-blind buggers in San Rafael old people's home who in the twilight of evening had taken her for a young and needy army recruit from the nearby Pedralbes barracks. But I persisted: 'Can't you give me any help at all, my angel?'

By this time I realised she wasn't going to give me anything of the kind, but I was trying to win time, because if she really was expecting a client, perhaps she would be so keen to get rid of me she would let something slip. I refused to budge therefore, alternately begging and threatening her for information. All at once, my sister became so agitated she poured the iced cocoa she was drinking all over my trousers. Aha! I thought, her client has arrived. I turned to see what he was like.

Unusually for one of my sister's clients, he was young and well built, with the physique of a bullfighter starting to run to seed. His attractive face had a certain duality to it, as if he were the child of Boris Karloff and Mae West. From his swaggering gait and clothing that was poorly suited to our climate, I could tell he was a sailor; his straw-blond hair and blue eyes suggested he was a foreigner, possibly Swedish. My sister often found customers among men of the sea. The fact that they came from distant lands meant they saw poor

Candida as something exotic and not as she really was – a blot on the landscape.

My sister had stood up and was slobbering all over the sailor, who was trying to fight her off as best he could. I decided to take advantage of the opportunity fate had cast my way to show off my English.

'Me, Candida, sister. Candida me sister, big fart. No, no big fart, big fuck. Strong. Not expensive. Ok?'

'Shut your trap,' the sailor replied in Spanish, obviously unimpressed. He spoke our language very well, and even had a slight Aragonese accent, which I found rather odd for a Swede.

My sister made a gesture which I took to mean 'clear off or I'll scratch your eyes out'. I took the hint, bid a fond farewell to the happy couple, and headed for the door. Things had not begun too well, but when do they ever? I resolved not to be downhearted, and turned my attention to finding a bed for the night. I knew of several cheap fleapits, but none of them were so cheap I could stay there for free, so I made my way back to Plaza Catalunya to try my luck on the metro. The sky had clouded over, and I could hear a distant rumble of thunder.

By now the cinemas and theatres were coming out, so the metro station was crowded with people. This made it easy for me to slip through and down onto the platform. When the first train pulled in, I sat in a first class compartment and tried to get some sleep. At Provenza station a gang of drunken youths got on and began to have fun at my expense. I played dumb and let them do what they liked. By the time they got off again at Tres Torres I had pocketed a wristwatch, two pens and a wallet. All I found in the wallet was an identity card, a driving licence, the photo of a girl, and a few credit cards. I threw the wallet away on a section of the line where I hoped they would never be found: that would teach their owner a lesson. I gleefully kept the watch and the pens, however, because they would enable me to pay for a hotel, to sleep between sheets, and at last have that refreshing shower.

While I was doing all this, the metro had reached the end of the line. I realised I wasn't far from the San Gervasio school run by the Lazarist nuns, and thought that, despite Inspector Flores' words of warning, it might be a good idea to take a look round. When I reached street level, I found it had started to drizzle. Coming across a copy of *La Vanguardia* in a nearby rubbish bin, I used it to cover my head.

Even though I pride myself on knowing Barcelona well, I took a couple of wrong turns before I finally came across the school: five years of confinement had dulled my sense of direction. By the time I reached the garden gate, I was soaked through. I soon discovered that the inspector's description had been accurate: both gate and walls seemed impregnable, although the way the street sloped down the hill meant the wall was slightly lower at the back of the property. That wasn't the worst of it: my brief, silent approach to the gate had not gone unnoticed by the mastiffs my friend the inspector had also spoken of. The pair of them had stuck their terrible jaws through the railings and were growling at me, uttering insults and no doubt calling my manhood into question in that animal language of theirs which science is as yet struggling in vain to comprehend.

The building that stood in the centre of the garden was large, and as far as the torrential rain and the darkness allowed me to judge, as ugly as sin. All the windows were narrow, apart from a pair of long stained-glass ones which must have been part of the chapel, although distance prevented me from being able to tell whether they were wide enough to permit a skinny body like that of an adolescent girl – or mine – to slip through. Two chimneys might have allowed access to a tiny person, except that they were right at the top of an impossibly steep roof. The neighbouring properties were also turn-of-the-century villas set in the midst of tree-filled gardens. I made a mental note of everything I saw, and judged that the moment had come for me to leave and seek some well-earned rest.

4

WHAT THE SWEDISH SAILOR DID NEXT

In spite of the lateness of the hour, the cafés on the Ramblas were packed. Because of the rain, which continued to pour down, the pavements outside were less crowded. I was reassured to see that in five years Barcelona hadn't changed much.

The hotel I was heading for was conveniently situated in an out-of-the-way corner of Calle de las Tapias. Outside, a neon light announced Hotel Cupido, all mod cons, bidet in every room. The receptionist was fast asleep, and was furious at being woken up. He was one-eyed, and apparently an expert in blasphemy. After some argument, he agreed to exchange the watch and pens for a room with a view for three nights only. When I protested, he argued that the current political instability had affected the influx of tourists and hit private investment. I countered by saying that if that was true for the hotel industry, it must also be valid for the watch and pen-making industries, to which the one-eyed receptionist replied that he couldn't give a stuff, and that three nights was his best offer, take it or leave it. His attitude was not exactly hospitable, but I had no choice but to accept. The room I was allotted was the size of a broom cupboard and stank of piss. The sheets were so filthy I had to prise them apart. Under the pillow I found a sock with holes in it. The shared bathroom looked more like a swimming-baths: the lavatory and the wash-basin were blocked, and in the latter floated a gooey purplish substance that was every fly's delight. Once again, I had no chance of a shower, so I headed back to my room. Through the walls I could hear people spitting, panting, and the occasional fart. I promised myself that if ever I became rich, I might do without other luxuries, but would make sure I always stayed in at least one-star hotels. As I was crushing the cockroaches scurrying across the bed, I could not help casting my mind back to my wonderfully hygienic cell in the asylum. I must confess I almost gave in to nostalgia. But eminent philosophers have argued that freedom is the supreme good, so who was I to call their judgement into question when I was at last enjoying said privilege? With this as consolation, I clambered into bed and tried to get to sleep. I repeated to myself silently the time I wanted to wake up the next morning, because I am aware that our unconscious, in addition to ruining our childhood, misrepresenting our emotions, reminding us of everything we would rather forget and revealing to us our innate misery – in other words, wrecking our lives – can also in compensation sometimes act as an alarm-clock.

I had almost drifted off when there was loud knocking at the door. Fortunately, this came equipped with a chain, which I had had the foresight to slip on before I got into bed. This meant that my visitor, whoever he might be and for whatever reason he might be outside, had to knock before entering. Thinking it might be some queer or other who wanted to make me a proposition, possibly involving money, I asked who it was. A voice I vaguely recognised responded:

'Let me in. I'm the boyfriend of your sister the hunchback.'

I opened the door a little way, and saw that the person standing there was none other than the young Swedish man I had met a few hours earlier with my sister, despite the fact that his muscular cheeks were no longer adorned by the blond beard he had sported earlier in the evening – or perhaps not, since although I have said I am a keen observer, sometimes this kind of detail escapes me – and that his clothes seemed rather more crumpled than I remembered.

'What can I do for you?' I asked.

'I want to come in,' the Swedish sailor said in a tremulous voice.

I hesitated a moment, but eventually opened the door for him, as he was not only a client of my sister's but even called himself her boyfriend, and I did not want to put her against me in any way. I thought that perhaps he wanted to discuss some family matter, and that as I was the male, he considered it best to talk to me. This anachronistic touch, as well as something in the Swede's manner, convinced me I was dealing with a decent, honest sort, although even more convincing was the pistol he drew from his pocket and pointed at me as he sat down on the bed. I am no great fan of weapons, or otherwise my career in crime would not have been so short and disastrous, and told him as such.

'My friend, I see,' I said, speaking slowly and trying to enunciate as clearly as possible so that the language barrier would not prove an obstacle to our mutual understanding, 'that something has led you to be suspicious of me: perhaps the natural mistrust my appearance arouses, or possibly a rumour spread by spiteful tongues. Yet I can assure you on my honour, on my sister's, as well as on our sainted mother's, God bless her, that you have nothing to fear from me. I am an observant man, and despite the fact that so far ours has been only a casual acquaintance, I have noticed that you are a man of principle, well educated, trustworthy, and of good birth, a person perhaps forced by the misfortunes of life to spend restless days in search of wider horizons, or even oblivion.'

My frank appeal did not appear to soften his attitude. He was still sitting on the bed, his eyes fixed on me and his face devoid of expression, his thoughts doubtless lost in goodness knows what painful memories, indescribable visions, what depths of melancholy.

'Of course, it may also be,' I went on, trying to rid him of any kind of suspicion that could make me a scapegoat for his anger, 'that you thought there is something more than a tie of kinship between my sister and me. Unfortunately, I have no documents to prove that we are indeed the latter. Sister and brother, I mean, a fact which would automatically shield us from any slanderous accusation. Nor can I point to any similarity in our appearance, as she is so beautiful, whereas I am nothing more than a heap of excrement. But isn't that what so often happens? Nature is capricious with her gifts, and nothing could be worse than making me pay for the fact that I lost out in the lottery of life, could it?'

This did not seem to have convinced him either, because he did not move a muscle, apart from taking off his jacket, which must have made him very hot. He sat there in his T-shirt, showing off the Herculean proportions of his chest and arms, among whose bulging muscles I would not have been in the least surprised to see the figure of the Virgin of Montserrat miraculously appear. I surmised he must be a fitness fanatic, one of those people who build their bodies thanks to a correspondence course, and buy weights, chest expanders and rowing machines to work out in their bedrooms. I decided to play on this aspect of his personality, probably caused by emotional insecurity, a fear of women, possibly even by doubts about his manhood.

'Nor would it make any sense, my friend, for you to use me, someone who not only plays no sport, but follows no diet – I don't even touch grapefruit, because I detest them – and on top of all that, smokes like a chimney, as a punch-bag, you who are the Tarzan of the seas, a worthy Scandinavian successor to the famous Charles Atlas, whom you may be too young to have known personally, but whose tiger-like knee-bends aroused such envy, and who stirred so many vain hopes in the breasts of the eight-stone weaklings of my generation, most of whom have now grown into twenty-stone couch potatoes.'

Whilst addressing him with these soothing words, I had been searching round the room for some heavy object to bash him on the head with, just in case my pleas did not succeed in changing his obviously hostile attitude. When I peered beneath the bed on which my taciturn future brother-in-law was sitting, in the hope of spying a chamber-pot I could use as a mallet (although of course in this wretched hotel there was no such thing) I saw a dark stain spreading between his legs. I put this down to a sudden bout of incontinence.

'You may even have thought,' I went on hurriedly, judging that while I was talking he did not seem inclined to make mincemeat of me, 'that when you saw us together I might be the pimp of your, if you will allow me the expression, beloved Candida. *No way!*' I emphasised the last words, to help his comprehension, which seemed slow to the point of being non-existent. 'You have to take my word for it, and my word is my bond, that this is a mistake, that Candida has never had recourse to such a despicable institution. No, she has always been a free agent, and her only crutch (forgive the comparison) has been Dr Sugrañes (I of course made this up, as my sister has never set foot in any doctor's surgery, being allergic as she is to the spoon handle they insist on poking into your mouth to inspect heaven knows what), who thanks to his deep knowledge has helped her and her clients avoid a whole host of problems. Allow me at this point to add that throughout my sister's career (inevitably short in one so young) she has never had the slightest trace of gonorrhoea, syphilis, the clap, or any nasty French disease. If by any chance you are toying with the idea of formalising before God and your fellow men a union which I perceive is already formalised in your hearts, you may rest assured that you could not have made a wiser choice. You can count not only on my consent, but my fraternal blessing.'

Smiling broadly, I went up to him, arms outstretched like the pope. When I saw he seemed to have no objection to my embrace, as soon as I got close enough I kneed him as hard as I could in his private parts. In spite of my being something of an expert at this, he did not react in the slightest. His eyes were still open wide, although by now they were no longer staring at me but into infinity. A greenish froth appeared on his lips. These details, plus the fact that he was no longer breathing, led me to conclude that he was dead. A closer inspection helped me ascertain that the puddle still spreading at his feet was blood, which had soaked the legs of his woollen trousers.

'What rotten luck,' I thought to myself, 'he seemed like a good catch for Candida.'

However, it was not so much this new reversal of our family fortunes which I had to ponder on, but the problem of how I was going to get rid of the body as quickly and discreetly as possible. I rejected the idea of pushing him out of the window, because it would have been obvious to whoever found him where he had come from. There was no sense either in trying to get him out through the hotel front door. I therefore decided on the simplest plan of action: to get rid of the body by leaving him where he was, and putting as much distance between him and me as possible. With any luck, when his corpse was found, they might think it was me and not the Swede in the bed. After all, I reasoned, the hotel porter was one-eyed. I began to search his pockets, and this is the inventory of what I found:

Left inside jacket pocket: nothing.

Right inside jacket pocket: nothing.

Left outside jacket pocket: nothing.

Right outside jacket pocket: nothing.

Left trouser pocket: a box of matches advertising a Galician restaurant, a 1,000 peseta banknote, and a torn, faded cinema ticket.

Right trouser pocket: a small transparent plastic bag containing a) three small packets of a white, alkaline substance with anaesthetic and narcotic properties, commonly known as cocaine; b) three strips of litmus paper impregnated with LSD; c) three amphetamine pills.

Shoes: nothing.

Socks: nothing.

Underpants: nothing.

Mouth: nothing.

Nasal, ear, and anal orifices: nothing.

While I was carrying out this search, my mind was racing with the questions I would have asked myself earlier if circumstances had permitted a moment's reflection. Who was this person anyway? There were no papers on his body, no diary, address book or any of those letters you slip into your pocket intending to reply to as soon as possible. Why had he come to see me? Given the fact that he was at death's door, his hypothetical interest in my sister hardly seemed a plausible explanation. How did he know where to find me? I had only come across somewhere to stay late on in the evening, so it was unlikely my sister or he knew where I would be that night. Why had he threatened me with a gun? Why was he carrying all those drugs in his trouser pocket? Why had he shaved off his beard? My sister was the only person who could answer these questions. I desperately needed to find and have a talk with her, even if that meant involving her in an affair which, to judge by the way it had begun, did not look to be very promising. I once again considered the possibility of returning to the asylum and reneging on the deal I had done with Inspector Flores, but surmised that my withdrawal could be interpreted as complicity in the Swedish sailor's death, or even leave me as the prime suspect. On the other hand, was I in any position to solve, not just the case or cases of the missing girls, but in addition that of the death of a stranger who for some unknown reason had taken it upon himself to come and give up the ghost on my bed?

What was clear was that I had no time to lose in idle thought. The one-eyed porter must have seen the Swede come in, and probably thought we were trying to share the room to avoid paying for its double occupation. This would mean he'd come up to investigate, which in turn meant he would soon discover the supposed stowaway's sad fate. I therefore decided to leave all theoretical considerations for some other time, transferred the contents of the dead man's pockets to mine (not forgetting the gun), made as little noise as possible as I opened the window, and tried to judge how far below the tiny interior courtyard was. It did not seem so distant I could not bridge it without too much trouble.

I laid the Swede out in my bed and closed his sea-blue eyes, which death had lent an air of surprised innocence, with two determined jabs of my fingers. I switched off the light, climbed out onto the ledge as best I could, then closed the window behind me. I spread my arms wide and launched myself into the dark void, only to discover – too late! – that the distance from window to ground was far greater than I had at first imagined, and that I was hurtling towards the fracture of several all-important bones, if not of my poor noggin itself, and consequently to the unfortunate end of all my adventures.

5

NOT ONE BUT TWO GREAT ESCAPES

Looping the loop as I fell, which brought to mind the aerial acrobatics of the unfortunate Prince Cantacuceno before his untimely death, my thoughts soon turned (I seemed to have time on my hands) to a growing certainty that on landing I would break my neck. The proof that this did not occur, however, is that you, dear reader, are able to read these enchanting pages. Instead, I landed in a deep, slimy pile of rubbish which, to judge by its smell and consistency, must have been made up of equal amounts of fish scraps, vegetables, fruit, salad, eggs, offal and other waste. I resurfaced covered from head to foot in a sticky, foul mess; yet I was pleased to find myself in one piece.

I picked my way through the flooded drains in the yard and reached a low wall, which I climbed without difficulty. As I straddled the top, I looked back one last time at the window of what had all too briefly been my room. It came as no surprise to see that the light was on, although I clearly remembered having switched it off. I could make out two silhouettes at the window. I wasted no time studying them, but leapt from the wall and ran off, dodging the sacks and crates piled on the ground. Another wall, or possibly the same one, rose before me. I have been scaling walls since childhood, so I dealt with this one like a seasoned steeple-chaser, and soon found myself in an alleyway at the far end of which I could see a street that led back to the Ramblas. Before I emerged into that quintessential Barcelona artery, I threw the gun down a drain, and was well pleased to see how the black hole swallowed the sinister artifact that only a few minutes earlier had been pointed straight at me. This was turning out to be my lucky night: it had even stopped raining.

My footsteps turned (because I turned them) towards the Leeches bar, where hours before I had met my sister and the unfortunate Swede. I hid in a doorway to keep watch on the entrance, trying not to tread in the seemingly endless pools of vomit spattered everywhere by English tourists whose stomachs had proved incapable of resisting the ravages of the night. I was waiting for my sister to appear. I was sure she would be inside, because she always ended up in the bar in the early hours in search of latecomers, clients so mean they hoped to pick up a bargain, which she was happy to offer them in her end-of-season remnants sale.

Rosy-fingered dawn was spreading across the sky by the time my sister finally emerged. It took me two strides to catch up with her, but she only gave me a scornful glance. I asked where she was going, she said she was heading home. I offered to escort her:

'Just looking at you,' I said, 'is an incitement to lose one's head. I can understand that men go crazy over you, but that does not mean, as your elder brother, that I am happy to condone it.'

'I already told you, I'm not giving you any money.'

I insisted once more that I had no intention of trying to scrounge or beg anything from her, and turned the talk to celebrity gossip I remembered from a two-year-old copy of *Hello!* magazine I had seen in the asylum. Candida did not seem to realise this was all old news, because high society lives are just as boring as ours, except that they are lived in considerably more luxury. At some point I dropped the following subtle question into my conversation:

'What happened to that admirable young man I had the pleasure of meeting not long ago and who was, if my eyes did not deceive me, so obviously enamoured of your charms?'

Candida spat disgustedly at a poster for the Liceo opera pasted on the wall.

'He left the way he came,' she said, adopting a sarcastic tone that could not conceal her indignation. 'He was sniffing round me for two whole days, and I'm still not sure what he was after. He wasn't my type, of course. I usually go with – how shall I put it? – sickos. I thought he must be one of those perverts who think that just because you are going through a bad patch you'll agree to anything: which, I have to admit, is a perfectly reasonable assumption. But anyway, it all came to nothing. Why do you ask?'

'No reason. I thought you two made a fine couple: you were both so young, so handsome, so full of life ... I've always thought you would end up making a home, Candida. This is no life for you: you deserve a family, children, an attentive husband, a holiday cottage in the mountains.'

I carried on with a minute description of the kind of happy family life poor Candida had not the slightest chance of ever knowing. What I said cheered her up no end, so that eventually she asked:

'Have you had breakfast?'

'I don't think so,' I said tactfully.

'Come home with me then; I've probably got some leftovers from last night.'

We set off down one of those streets redolent of old Barcelona, the sort that only needs a roof to turn it into a sewer. We came to a halt outside a blackened, dilapidated block of flats. Out of the doorway shot a lizard chewing on a beetle as it struggled in the mouth of a rat that was being chased by a cat. We climbed the staircase, lighting our way with matches that were blown out almost at once by the draft coming in through the smashed windows on the house front. When we reached her door, my sister, who was gasping for breath because of her asthma, turned the key in the lock and exclaimed:

'That's odd! I could have sworn I double-locked it when I left. I must be growing old.'

'Don't talk nonsense, Candida. You're a pure rosebud still,' I said almost without thinking, because I was also busy worrying about the lock. I was right to be concerned, because no sooner had Candida flicked on the switch and light invaded the tiny room which was all she could call home (the toilet was in the stairwell, which also served as a landing) than we found ourselves face to face with the Swede, the very same Swede I had left sleeping the sleep of the just in my bed. Now here he was, staring at us with those sea-blue eyes of his from an armchair positioned in the centre of the room, just as if this were a village and he were the visiting priest. Poor Candida stifled a cry of panic.

'Don't be frightened, Candida,' I said, making sure the door was closed behind our backs. 'He won't do anything to you.'

'Maybe not, but what is this guy doing here?' my sister whispered, as though worried the Swede might overhear us. 'Why does he look so serious? Why doesn't he move?'

'I can give you a definite answer to the second question. I've no idea about the first, except to tell you I'm sure he didn't choose to be here. Did he know your address?'

'No, how could he?'

'You might have given it him.'

'I never tell clients where I live. What if there's something ...' she pointed at the unmoving Swede, casting a worried glance in my direction.

'Wrong with him? Yes, you're right. Let's get out of here before it's too late.'

It already was. Hardly had I uttered these prophetic words when there came a loud hammering at the door and a manly voice shouted:

'Police! Open up or we'll break the door down!'

These words served only to demonstrate the lack of grammatical accuracy to be found among our security forces nowadays, as no sooner had they been uttered than three policemen, an inspector in plain clothes and two uniformed officers, knocked down the rickety door, rushed in brandishing guns and truncheons, and shouted almost in unison:

'Don't move! You're all under arrest!'

This did seem grammatically clear, and so my sister and I decided the best thing would be to put our hands up. My fingers ended caught in the cobwebs which hung from the ceiling beams like a canopy. When they saw we were offering no resistance, the two uniforms proceeded to search my sister's humble home, smashing all her crockery with their truncheons, kicking the few pieces of furniture over, and relieving themselves on the sheets of her tattered mattress. While they were thus occupied, the inspector, grinning so broadly I could see his gold teeth, bridges, crowns, fillings and a bad attack of tartar, demanded we identify ourselves, with the following pithy phrase:

'Who the fuck are you two?'

My sister obediently showed him her identity card. Unfortunately, she had scratched out the date of birth with a razor blade, which led the inspector to laugh in a very cruel manner, and comment:

'Pull the other one.'

By this time, the two uniforms had discovered the corpse, satisfied themselves that he was in fact dead, searched him thoroughly, and then shouted to their superior:

'Hey chief, we've caught 'em red 'anded.'

The inspector made no reply, as he was still insisting that I prove my identity. I found this somewhat difficult, as the only thing I had in my pocket was not my identity card but a plastic bag stuffed with drugs. I resolved to go for broke and to use a tried and trusted stratagem.

'My friend,' I said slowly, but loud enough for all three of them to hear, 'you don't know what you're getting yourself into.'

'What the fuck?' replied the inspector incredulously.

'Come closer, kid,' I said, lowering my arms as I did so, partly to regain at least a shred of dignity, and partly to disguise the stench from my armpits, which did little to help my cause. 'Have you any idea who you are talking to?'

'A stinking clown.'

'A clever deduction, and yet an incorrect one. Inspector, you are speaking to none other than Don Ceferino Sugrañes, city councillor and the owner of banks, property companies, insurance, finance and building firms, as well as registry offices and courts, to name only a few of the sidelines I am involved in. As you, thanks to the intelligence that comes with your position, will doubtless realise, this means I am not the kind of person to carry any form of identity on him, not merely out of fear of what our punctilious electorate might think if they saw me like this, but also to avoid the detectives that my lady wife, who is currently suing for divorce, has set upon me, but which I can prove – my identity that is, thanks to my chauffeur, bodyguard and manager (this last title coming from the fact that for tax reasons there are certain shady concerns in which I have no wish to see my own name involved), who at this very moment is waiting for me on the street corner with strict instructions to inform the Prime Minister if I do not emerge safe and sound within ten minutes from this hellhole, to which I was lured by the hag you see before you, who alone is responsible for this dilemma in which in all innocence I find myself embroiled, this treacherous harpy who brought me here to rob, blackmail, sodomise and commit other heinous crimes against my person – even though, as I can see she is already doing, she will try to deny all of this, which only goes to prove the truth of my assertions, because who would you rather believe, Inspector, if you had to choose: an honest citizen like me, a captain of industry, scion of the thrusting Catalan bourgeoisie, an emblem of Spain and its glorious empire, or this misshapen, decrepit old bag whose breath is so foul it could drop a fly at a hundred paces, a professional whore to boot – something easily proven if you should care to inspect her bag, where you will find several not exactly unused condoms, and whom I had promised, in return for services which I see no reason to detail here and now, the exorbitant sum of 1,000 pesetas, these very same 1,000 pesetas I am now handing to you, inspector, as documentary proof of my allegations.'

At this, I took the 1,000-peseta note I had found on the Swede out of my pocket and gave it to the inspector. As he stood there uncertain as to what to do with the money, I head-butted him on the nose, from which blood started to pour. He grimaced with pain and made an attempt to curse, but by this time I was already leaping over the smashed door and heading as quickly as I could down the stairs, with the two uniforms in close pursuit. I had enough breath left to shout:

'Don't pay any attention to what I said about you, Candida! It was all a trick!' I didn't really hold out much hope that she could hear me above all the din, or even that she would believe me if she did catch any of it.

Out in the street, I saw the pavements were full of workers wending their weary way to work, and since the two uniforms were still close on my heels, and thanks to their better physiques, training and greater enthusiasm for the task looked to be on the point of collaring me, I started to shout at the top of my voice:

'Long live the anarchist trade union! Long live the workers!'

The reaction was immediate: the lines of workers all raised their fists and began to shout similar slogans. As I had hoped, the policemen also reacted. They had obviously not yet become accustomed to the political liberalisation taking place in Spain since the death of the Generalissimo, and laid all about them with their truncheons. Under cover of the ensuing battle, I made good my escape.

Now that my pursuers had been put off the scent and I was able to breathe more freely, I reviewed my situation. It seemed to me it could hardly be worse. There was only one person who could help me and help save my sister from a long spell in jail. I therefore rang Inspector Flores from a public phone box, which, since I found myself penniless yet again, I had to force with a piece of wire. Despite the early hour, Flores was already at his desk. At first he seemed surprised to hear me, but once I had told him everything that had happened, including my escape from the police (although I admit that at this point I slightly modified the details) the tone of his voice changed from one of surprise to anger.

'You mean to say, you worm, that you haven't found out a single thing about that missing girl yet?' he roared, the questions clawing at my ear. I had almost completely forgotten about the missing girl. I muttered a few clumsy excuses and promised to set to work on the case (or cases) at once.

'Look here, my son,' the inspector replied, in such a gentle way I was completely taken aback. I had never heard him use the word 'son' about me unless it was followed by 'of a bitch'. 'Why don't we say you'll drop this business? Perhaps I made a mistake in confiding such a difficult task to you. We mustn't forget that you are still ... convalescing, and that all the effort required might only worsen your ... condition. Why don't you come down to Headquarters so we can talk about it calmly over a couple of refreshing Pepsis?'

I have to admit that this unaccustomed kid-glove treatment had a mesmeric effect on me, and that Inspector Flores' words and the kindness with which they were said almost brought tears to my eyes; and yet this didn't mean I was unaware of his ulterior motive, namely, to entice me down to police headquarters in order to have me sent back to the asylum scarcely twenty-four hours after my release. I therefore replied in the firm but polite tone normally reserved for getting rid of Jehovah's witnesses that I had not the slightest intention of abandoning the case, not because I gave a fig for what might have happened to some silly girl, but because my freedom depended on it.

'I didn't ask your opinion, you clown!' snarled Inspector Flores, who suddenly appeared to have regained his usual manner. 'Either you get down here now of your own accord or I'll bring you in handcuffed, and you'll be treated like the common criminal you are genetically and by profession. Do you hear me, animal?'

'Yes, I hear you, Inspector sir,' I replied, 'but with all due respect I am not going to follow your advice, because I am determined to prove my capabilities and my sanity to society, even if I have to die in the attempt. And I must warn you, again with all due respect, that you should make no attempt to trace this call as I'm sure you've seen it done in films, first, because it's not possible, second because I'm calling from a public phone box, and third, because I'm going to hang up right now, just in case.'

Which I did. This time it did not take me long to realise that, far from improving, my situation had taken yet another turn for the worse, and not only that, but seemed likely to deteriorate still further. I therefore decided to concentrate all my energies on searching for the missing girl and to post-pone unravelling the mystery of the Swedish sailor until a better occasion presented itself.

6

THE MERRY GARDENER

As a first precaution, I headed for a small side-street off Calle Tallers where I knew a medical clinic piled its waste. I was hoping to find something that would help me disguise my identity – some unwanted bit of a cadaver, for example, which I could somehow attach to my features to change them. My luck was out, and the best I could do was rescue a few strands of not-too-filthy cotton wool. Winding this round a piece of string I also found, I gave myself the bushy beard of a patriarch, which not only concealed my features, but lent me a respectable, even imposing air. Thus disguised, I sneaked into the metro a second time, and headed once more for the neighbourhood where the San Gervasio school was situated.

On my way there I flicked through a magazine I had filched from the station kiosk, which from the bloody photos on the cover I thought must be devoted to the latest crimes. I was looking for news of the Swedish sailor's death, and whatever details the reporter might have been able to discover about it. There was nothing. Instead, there was page after page of women in the buff. 'Ilsa just loves the sun!' declared a feature article that had more pictures than text. Ilsa's ivory thighs, alabaster breasts and flinty buttocks burst out all over a miraculously deserted Costa Brava. I guessed that either the photo was taken in winter or it was a painted backdrop. According to Ilsa, we Spaniards were a sexy lot. I left the magazine on the seat, and peered into the grimy window opposite me. The image I could see was of someone who was neither young nor good-looking, and not exactly sexy either. I sighed a deep sigh.

'Oh, Ilsa my love,' I was thinking, 'Where are you when I need you?'

The metro reached the station. I got out, made my way up to street level, and this time found the school at the first attempt.

From my previous evening's reconnoitring, I had concluded that such a well-kept garden must depend on the services of a full-time gardener. I had further reasoned that such a person, who was at the same time both part and yet not part of the religious community, might be my first line of approach in the task of resolving the mystery. It also occurred to me that someone who spent their life in such austere surroundings would not be averse to receiving some small gift. To this end, I had taken advantage of a shop assistant's momentary lack of vigilance to purloin a bottle of wine, which I hid under the folds of my shirt. However, as I came within sight of the forbidding walls of the chaste educational establishment, I surmised that whilst wine may have a profound effect on human behaviour, it takes far too long to do so. I therefore opened the bottle, which was easy enough, since it had a plastic top, and, taking from my pocket the bag of drugs the Swede had bequeathed me, I quickly poured the cocaine, amphetamine pills and the LSD into the wine. I swirled the mixture round, hid the bottle inside my shirt again, and then headed straight for my target. I found him close to the wide-open garden gate, busy with some horticultural task or other. The gardener was a rather rough-looking young man. He was pruning a bed of beautiful flowers, singing quietly to himself. He greeted me with the kind of grunt that suggested he had no wish to be interrupted.

'Bless the Lord for such a fine day,' I said, refusing to be put off by his gruff reception. 'Would I by any chance be speaking to the gardener of this magnificent mansion?'

He nodded, waving the shears he was carrying at me, although quite possibly without malice. I smiled at him.

'In that case, I can count myself fortunate,' I said. 'I've come a long way to meet you. First, may I introduce myself? I am Don Arborio Sugrañes, professor in Green Studies at the University of France. And may I also say by way of introduction that you may not be aware of this, but your garden here is famous throughout the world. After all my years of study, I felt that before I retire I just had to meet the person whose efforts, skill and diligence have made this miracle possible. As a token of my admiration and gratitude, would you accept, maestro, a libation from this bottle of wine I have brought especially from my country for the occasion?'

I pulled out the wine, half of which had already spilled all over my shirt and beard. I offered it to the gardener, who snatched it greedily and immediately changed his tone.

'You should have said that straight off,' he growled, 'What the fuck do you want anyway?'

'First and foremost,' I replied, 'for you to slake your thirst drinking my health.'

'This wine has a strange taste, doesn't it?'

'That's because it's a very special vintage. There are only two bottles like it in the whole world.'

'Here it says "Pentavin, table wine",' objected the gardener, pointing to the label.

I gave him a knowing wink.

'The border customs ... if you know what I mean,' I said, hoping to gain time so that the brew could have its effect. I could tell by his pupils and his voice that this wouldn't take long. 'Is something wrong, my friend?'

'My head's started spinning.'

'That must be the summer sun. How do the nuns treat you?'

'I could complain, but I won't. There's so much unemployment around ...'

'Yes indeed, these are hard times. I suppose you must know everything that goes on inside the school, don't you?'

'I know a little, but I keep my mouth shut. If you're some trade union Johnny, I'm not saying a word. Do you mind if I take my shirt off?'

'Make yourself at home. Is the unkind gossip about the school true?'

'Help me untie my shoe laces. What gossip would that be?'

'That girls go missing from the dormitories. I don't believe any such thing, of course. Would you like me to take off your socks while I'm at it?'

'Yes please, they seem very tight. What were you saying?'

'That girls go missing at night.'

'Yes, that's true. But I have nothing to do with it.'

'I wasn't suggesting you did. But why do you think those sweet little angels disappear?'

'How should I know? They're probably pregnant, the dirty little beggars.'

'Do things like that go on inside the school?'

'Not that I know of. If I were given half a chance, they would.'

'Why don't I take those shears from you? We don't want you to hurt yourself, or to prune me by accident, do we? But do go on telling me the story about the disappearance.'

'I know nothing about that. Why are there so many suns all of a sudden?'

'Probably a miracle. Tell me about the other girl, the one who vanished six years ago.'

'You know about that too?'

'That and a lot more besides. But what exactly happened six years ago?'

'No idea. I wasn't here then.'

'So who was?'

'My predecessor. A crazy old man. They had to get rid of him.'

'When?'

'Six years ago: that's how long I've been working here.'

'Why did they sack him?'

'For indecent behaviour. I suspect he was one of those dirty old men who like to open their flies in front of young girls. Look, here's a present for you: you can have my trousers.'

'That's very kind of you. What an elegant line they have. What was the other gardener's name?'

'Cagomelo Purga. Why do you ask?'

'Just answer my questions. Where can I find him? What does he do these days?'

'Nothing, I should imagine. You'll find him at home. I know he used to live in Calle de la Cadena, but I can't remember the number.'

'Where were you the night the girl disappeared?'

'Six years ago?'

'No, my friend, a couple of days ago.'

'I don't know. Watching TV in a bar, or visiting a whorehouse ... I must have been doing something.'

'How can you possibly not remember? Hasn't Inspector Flores tried to refresh your memory – like this?' With that, I slapped him as hard as I could on both cheeks. He burst into giggles.

'The cops?' he said, roaring with laughter. 'The cops? I haven't had anything to do with them since the time I strangled that Algerian bastard a few years back. The Arab dog!' he said, spitting into the oleanders.

'How many years ago?'

'It must have been six. I'd already forgotten all about that. Isn't it strange how wine refreshes your memory and sharpens your senses? Now, for example, I can feel my whole body swaying to the rhythm of those ancient trees. I'm in touch with the whole of nature. Everything is so wonderful! Could you spare me another mouthful, kind sir?'

I let him finish the bottle, because what he had just told me had left me perplexed. How could it be that someone normally so meticulous as Inspector Flores hadn't interrogated the gardener, especially as he apparently had a criminal record? When I raised my head to ponder the question more fully, my eyes lit on a balcony on the second floor of the school. There I spied the stern figure of the Mother Superior, whom as you will doubtless remember I had met at the asylum the previous day. Not only was she staring straight at me, but she was waving her arms about and saying something that distance prevented me hearing. Two other figures immediately joined her on the balcony. At first I thought they must be novices, but soon, when I spotted their leather belts and sub-machine guns, realised they were cops. The nun turned to them, and then pointed at me in an accusing manner. The cops turned on their heels and disappeared from the balcony.

I was not too worried by this. By this time, the gardener was wearing his underpants on his head and chanting mantras. It was easy enough for me to lead him towards the gate.

I waited until the uniforms came rushing out of the school front door, then shouted to him:

'Run, there's a toad on your tail!'

Terrified, the gardener shot out of the gate, while I bent over the flower bed and started lopping off flowers as fast as I could with the pair of shears I had taken from him moments before. As I had calculated, the two uniforms raced off after the gardener, paying no attention to the desperate gestures the Mother Superior made at them from the balcony. I waited until the fugitive and the two cops had disappeared up the street, then deposited my fake beard on a rosebush, and strolled off in the opposite direction. Before I left the school grounds, I made sure to raise my arms and shrug in the direction of the distraught nun, as though to say:

'Forgive the intrusion, but don't lose faith in me. I'm still on the case.'

As I headed for the metro station, I heard the rat-a-tat-tat of a machine gun in the distance. And, since this chapter has turned out rather short, I will make use of the remaining space to deal with a question which is probably on the minds of all readers who have accompanied me thus far, namely, what my name is. This is something that demands an explanation.

When I was born, my mother, who could not permit herself any other indiscretions for fear of my father, was, like every other woman of her generation, hopelessly and, it has to be said, unrequitedly in love with Clark Gable. When I came to be baptised, she insisted in the middle of the ceremony that I was to be called Gonewiththewind. Naturally enough, the very idea filled the priest officiating at the rite with horror. The argument soon turned into a brawl and my godmother, who needed both hands to hit her husband (a daily routine with those two) left me floating in the font, in whose waters I would most certainly have drowned, had it not been for ... but that's another story, which is leading us away from the narrative line we are following. In any case, this is a false dilemma, as my real, complete name is only to be found in the infallible police archives, while on a daily basis I am usually referred to as 'toe-rag', 'rat', 'piece of shit', 'poofter' and other descriptions so various and abundant they prove not only the boundless creativity of the human mind but the inexhaustible riches of our language.

7

THE SAINTLY GARDENER

Calle de la Cadena is not long, so it was not hard for me to find out exactly where the former school gardener lived. All his neighbours seemed to know and like him. I learnt, too, that he had lost his wife some time earlier and lived on his own, in straitened circumstances. During the bullfighting season he earned a few pennies sweeping up dung from the Monumental bullring and selling it to farmers out in the Prat region; in winter he depended almost entirely on charity. Don Cagomelo Purga received me very warmly. His dwelling was one ramshackle room in which were crammed a narrow camp bed, a bedside table piled high with yellowing magazines, a table and two chairs, a door-less wardrobe and an electric hotplate where a pan was boiling. I asked for the bathroom, as I needed a pee. He pointed to the tiny window in one wall.

'Out of consideration for any passers-by,' he said, 'when you feel it coming, shout "Ahoy there!" and make sure the last drops fall outside too: uric acid is bad for floor tiles, and I'm too old to be scrubbing them day and night. If the window's too high, use a chair. I used to piss like a horse, but now I can hardly get it out. Years ago we used to have a really funny chamber pot, a design with a motto that read "I can see you". My dear late-lamented wife used to laugh fit to burst whenever she saw it. When God called her to his side, I insisted they bury it with her. That pot was the only gift I could give her in thirty years of married life, and it would have felt like a betrayal to go on using it without her. The window is good enough for me. If it's not just a piss you need, things can get rather complicated, but practice makes perfect, don't you agree?'

Hating pretension as I do, I was pleased at the gardener's directness. While I was busy emptying my bladder, he returned to the task I had interrupted. When I turned back towards him, I could see he was at the table trying to stick together the pieces of his set of false teeth with glue.

'I broke it yesterday against the back of a pew in church,' he explained. 'Divine punishment; I fell asleep during mass. Are you religious?'

'My life is one of pure devotion to the church.'

'There can be no greater recommendation in this world or the next. How may I be of service to you?'

'I'll come straight to the point. I understand you were once the gardener at the girls' school in San Gervasio.'

'Ah yes, the happiest time of my life. When I first got there, what is now a beautiful garden was a wild jungle. With God's helping hand, I converted it into an earthly paradise.'

'Yes, one of the finest I've seen. But why was it so over-grown?'

'The property had been abandoned for years. Would you like something to drink, señor?'

'Sugrañes. Fervoroso Sugrañes, at your and God's service. You wouldn't by any chance have some Pepsi-Cola, would you?'

'No, I'm sorry. My circumstances do not permit me such luxuries. I can offer you tap water or, if you prefer, you can share some of the spinach soup I was making.'

'That's very kind of you, but I've just had lunch,' I lied, feeling embarrassed about taking what little he had from him. 'What was the school before it became a school?'

'I told you, nothing. An abandoned mansion.'

'And before that?'

'I've no idea. I was never curious enough to find out. Are you an estate agent then?'

From his question I could tell that this somewhat marginal aficionado of the tauromachial art must have problems with his eyes.

'Tell me about your job at the school. Did you say you were well paid?'

'Not a bit of it. When I said they were the happiest days of my life, I wasn't referring to money matters. The nuns paid below the minimum wage, never signed me up for social security, and didn't contribute to my pension. I was happy because I liked my job and because I was able to go to the chapel when the girls weren't there.'

'Didn't you have any contact with the girls?'

'On the contrary. At break-time I always had to keep watch to make sure they weren't ruining my flowers. They were little devils: they stole acid from the school lab and threw it on the flower beds. Or they would hide bits of glass in the soil so I would cut myself. Like I say, they were little devils.'

'But you like children, don't you?'

'Yes, a lot. They're God's blessing.'

'But you don't have any?'

'My wife and I never consummated our marriage. We were old fashioned in that way. People nowadays marry just so they can have a bit of hanky-panky. No, I shouldn't say that: "Judge not and ye shall not be judged." God knows, sometimes it was hard for us to resist temptation. Just imagine – thirty years sleeping together in this narrow bed. But the Almighty gave us strength. Whenever it seemed our passion was about to overwhelm us I would beat my wife with my belt, and she would bash me on the head with the iron.'

'Why did you stop doing it? Your job at the school, I mean.'

'The nuns decided to pension me off. I felt fine, never better, and still do, thanks be to God, but they never asked me. One day the Mother Superior called me in and said: "Cagomelo, you've just retired, I hope you enjoy your retirement." They gave me an hour to collect my things and leave.'

'They must have paid you decent compensation.'

'Not a penny. They gave me a portrait of the holy father

who founded the school, and a year's subscription to the school magazine, *Roses for Mary*.'

He pointed to a picture hanging over his bed, which showed a man dressed in red who looked surprisingly like The Hulk. Rays of light poured from the saint's head. The copies of the magazine were the ones I had seen piled high on the bedside table when I came in.

'I glance at them before I go to sleep. They have short prayers and inspiring stories for the month of May. Would you like to have a read?'

'I'd love to, but some other time. Is it true that just before you retired there was a strange incident at the school? Did a girl die or something?'

'Die? No, may the Holy Virgin forbid. She disappeared for a few days, but her guardian angel returned her safe and sound.'

'Did you know the child?'

'Isabelita? Of course! She was a little devil.'

'Isabelita Sugrañes a little devil?'

'Isabelita Peraplana. You're Sugrañes, I seem to remember.'

'I've got a niece called that – Isabelita after her mother, and Sugrañes after her father and me. Sometimes I get confused. Tell me about her.'

'Isabelita Peraplana? What is there to say? She was the prettiest girl in her class ... how shall I put it? The most virginal. She was the nuns' favourite, an example for all the others to follow. She studied hard and was very devout.'

'Yet she was a little devil?'

'No, not Isabelita. It was the other one who led her on, and she was so innocent she would follow.'

'Which other one?'

'Mercedes.'

'Mercedes Sugrañes?'

'No, wrong again. Mercedes Negrer was her name. They were best friends, but completely different! Do you have a moment? I'll show you the photos.'

'You have photos of the girls?'

'Of course, in the magazines.'

I went over to the bedside table and came back with an armful of magazines.

'Look for the one dated April 1971. My eyesight isn't what it used to be.'

I found the issue he had mentioned, and flicked through the pages until I came to a section called "Flowers from our Garden". This showed a half-page photograph of each class, drawn up on the steps of the chapel in rows.

'Look for the fifth form. Have you found it? Let me see.'

He brought the magazine up so close to his face I was afraid he might poke his eye out. When he held it away again, the paper was smeared with saliva.

'This is Isabelita, the blonde girl on the back row. Mercedes Negrer is standing next to her, on the left – on the left in the magazine, not on your left, I mean. Can you spot them?'

For some strange reason, the photograph of the fifth form made me feel vaguely sad. I had a sudden mental flash of Ilsa and her monumental body, splashing her attractions all along our rocky coast while she passed judgement on our weary race.

'Yes, she certainly is pretty. I can see you had good taste.'

I tried to fix the image of Isabelita Peraplana in my mind. Then I handed him back the magazine and said with feigned innocence:

'Why did you show me the photo of the fifth form? I was never much of a student, but I seem to remember that in those days you had to do six years before you took your exams, didn't you?'

'You've got a good memory. Six years, then sixth form college. Isabelita never took her exams.'

'Why was that? Didn't you say she studied hard?'

'Yes, she was the best student. The truth is, I don't know what happened. As I told you, I left the school that same year, and never heard anything more from the girls. For a while I was hoping some of them might pay me a visit, but they never did.'

'How do you know then that Isabelita didn't finish?'

'Because she's not in the next year's photograph. The nuns gave me a subscription, remember.'

'Could I check that for myself?'

'Be my guest.'

I found the 1972 magazine, and the photo of the sixth year. From what the Mother Superior had told me in the asylum, I was not surprised to find that Isabelita was not there. No, I was looking for something else, and my suspicions were confirmed: Mercedes Negrer had also disappeared from the class photo. Although everything was still very confused, the pieces of the jigsaw were beginning to fall into place. I put the pile of magazines back on the table and said goodbye to the hospitable gardener, thanking him for his kindness.

'At your service,' he said. 'There's just one thing I'd like to ask you, if it's not too much trouble.'

'Of course.'

'Why did you come?'

'I've heard that the gardener's job at the school is vacant again. I thought you might be interested, if the idea appeals to you. If it does, go to the school in a couple of days. But don't tell them I sent you: there might be problems with the unions.'

'We lived better under Franco,' muttered the aged gardener.

'You never spoke a truer word,' I agreed.

8

PREMARITAL TENSION

The Peraplana family home, which I found thanks to the phone directory – there were only two Peraplanas listed, and the other one was a travelling salesman who lived in La Verneda – was the only villa left in Calle Reina Cristina Eugenía. All the others had been turned into luxury red-brick apartments, with huge windows and impressive entrance halls, where doormen in a wide array of coloured uniforms stood guard. A small group of maids, also in uniform, had gathered outside one of these imposing entrances. Adopting the cocky swagger I knew went down well with the weaker sex, I strolled over to them.

'Hi there, girls,' I said seductively.

My chat-up line was rewarded with giggles and titters.

'Look who's here,' said one of them: 'It's Frankenstein's monster.'

I let them laugh at me for a while, then put on my saddest face. By pinching my balls on the sly I even managed to shed a few tears. The maids, who when it came down to it were all heart, took pity on me and asked what was wrong.

'It's a very sad story, which I'll tell you if you insist. My name is Toribio Sugrañes, and I did my national service with Señor Peraplana, the man who lives up there in that lovely villa. He was training to be a lieutenant while I was a squaddie. One day in the camp a mule on heat was about to give Peraplana a tremendous kick; I leapt in between them and saved his life, at the cost of this missing tooth you see here. As you can imagine, Peraplana was extremely grateful, and swore that if ever I needed anything, I only had to ask. Many years have gone by since then, and as you can perhaps tell from my appearance, I am going through a difficult patch. I remembered his promise, so this morning I came to knock on his door to remind him of it: but what do you think happened? Do you think he opened his arms to me? Not a bit of it! All I got from him was a kick in the pants!'

'What did you expect, dummy?' scoffed one of the maids.

'Were you born yesterday?' asked another.

'I bet he thinks storks bring babies,' laughed a third.

'Don't make fun of him,' said the one who appeared most sensible of them all, a sixteen-year-old as pert as a cherry on a cake. 'All rich people are bastards. My boyfriend told me so: he's a Socialist.'

'Don't be in such a hurry to condemn,' said a fifth maid, whose short uniform gave an appetising glimpse of a pair of juicy hams. 'It's been a long time since the mule incident – and it seems as if the years have been kinder to you than to Señor Peraplana. Are you sure you did military service together?'

'Yes, but I did it straight from school, and Peraplana managed to avoid it for as long as possible. That would explain the age difference that you so cleverly noticed, sweetheart.'

This improvised explanation seemed to satisfy Miss Hammy. She went on:

'I've heard the Peraplana family is decent enough. They pay well and don't create problems. It could be that everything in the house is upside down at the moment because of their daughter's wedding.'

'Isabelita is getting married?' I asked.

'Did she do military service with you too?' asked Miss Hammy. Her powers of deduction made her a danger to me.

'When he was on leave after swearing allegiance, he got his girlfriend in Salou pregnant, so as soon as we'd done our time there was a shotgun wedding. He told me that if it was a girl they were going to call her Isabelita. How time flies! And how I'd like to see their daughter now! It brings back so many memories!'

'Well I don't think they'll invite you to the wedding, pugface,' the Socialist's girlfriend chimed in. 'They say the fiancé is rolling in it.'

'Is he good looking as well?' another one wanted to know.

'Like a TV presenter,' said Miss Cupcake.

Time was getting on, and all the maids suddenly dispersed like a flock of pigeons which, startled into the air by a sudden noise, crap on you to lighten their load. I was left alone in the middle of the street, which at that time of day was very quiet. I stood there for a few moments, going over a plan that required me yet again to make use of the nearby refuse bins, which for me had become a handy substitute for Marks & Spencers. A box, some wrapping paper, a piece of string and other bits and pieces were enough for me to create a convincing package. I tucked it under my arm and set off for the Peraplana house. I walked up a gravel path where two Seats and a Renault were parked, through a refreshing garden in which a marble fountain, a swing, and a white table with a tilted parasol had pride of place. I stopped at the leaded-glass front door and pushed the bell, which emitted a pleasant two-tone ding-dong. When a portly butler answered, I greeted him effusively.

'I'm from Sugrañes' Jewellers in Paseo de Gracia,' I said. 'I've brought a wedding present for Señorita Isabel Peraplana. Is she at home?'

'Yes, but she can't see you now,' said the butler. 'Leave the parcel with me, and I'll see she gets it.'

He fished a couple of coins out of his pocket, and I was so hungry I half-wondered whether it wouldn't be simpler just to grab them and get out of there as quickly as possible. I soon dismissed this ignoble thought, and twisted round to make sure the butler could not get hold of the package.

'She has to sign for it,' I said.

'I'm authorised to do so on her behalf,' the snooty butler replied.

'But I'm not authorised to hand the package over unless

Señorita Isabel Peraplana signs it herself, with me as witness. It's a house rule.'

My resolute attitude gave the butler pause for thought.

'As I already told you, the señorita cannot come out at this moment: she is trying on her wedding dress.'

'Okay, why don't we do this?' I suggested. 'You call the shop, and if they give the say-so, I'm more than happy to accept not your signature but your word as a gentleman.'

My plausible idea seemed to sway the butler, who allowed me inside the house. I prayed to all the saints that there would not be a phone in the hall, and my prayers were answered. The hall was a circular room with a high, domed ceiling. There was hardly any furniture, apart from palm-trees in tubs and some bronze statues of naked trollops and romping dwarfs. The butler signed for me to wait for him there while he made the phone call from the 'office'. I'd always thought that meant some kind of urinal, but I didn't allow my surprise to show. When he asked what the jeweller's number was, I said I couldn't remember.

'Look in the directory under Sugrañes' Jewellers. If that's not it, try Jewellers: Sugrañes, and if that's not there either, try "antique and new jewellery", Sugrañes family. And make sure you ask for the elder Sugrañes. His son is mentally handicapped and incapable of making any decisions.'

As soon as the butler had disappeared, I ran up the carpeted stairs at the far end of the hall. When I reached the first floor, I began sticking my head round all the doors I came to. At the third attempt, I struck lucky: inside were two people, one a middle-aged woman I decided must be the dressmaker since she was wearing a small pincushion on her arm like a corporal's stripes. Despite the six years that had passed between the photograph the virtuous gardener had shown me and the person now in front of me, I immediately recognised the other figure as Isabel Peraplana, who had grown into a young woman beautiful enough to cause a train-wreck. Her blonde hair flowed down onto her delicate shoulders, and was crowned with a diadem of white flowers. Apart from this, all she was wearing were a tiny white bra and a pair of lace panties that gave a tantalising glimpse of some little blonde curls. To complete the picture, I should say that both women had their mouths wide open and were issuing shouts of terror caused in no small measure by my sudden intrusion.

'I've brought a beautiful gift from Sugrañes' Jewellers,' I hastened to say, rattling the fake package with the two sardine tins I had put inside. Not even this succeeded in calming the two women. In a last desperate effort, I went up to the dressmaker and growled:

'I'll gobble you up, big tits!'

At this, she rushed out into the corridor, leaving behind her a trail of pins like Tom Thumb and his breadcrumbs, and screaming for help at the top of her voice. Once she had gone, I slammed the door shut and turned the key. I turned back to face Isabelita Peraplana, who was staring at me in mute horror while she tried to cover her charms with her hands: if I had not had such an important message to deliver, the sight would have driven me wild.

'Señorita Peraplana,' I gabbled, 'we only have a few

seconds. Try to listen carefully to what I'm going to say. I'm not a delivery boy from Sugrañes' Jewellers; in fact, I doubt if such a firm even exists. All this package contains are a few empty tins, put there with the sole aim of gaining entrance into this house, a liberty I have taken in order to talk to you in private. You have nothing to fear from me. I am a former delinquent, who was freed only yesterday. The police are after me so they can shut me up in the asylum again, because they think I was involved in the death of a man – or perhaps two, if the machine-gun fire I heard was on target. I'm also caught up in an affair of drug-trafficking: cocaine, amphetamines and LSD. And my poor whore of a sister is in the clink because of me. So you see what a dramatic situation I find myself in. I insist though that you have nothing to fear: I'm not crazy like they claim, and I'm no criminal. It's true I may smell of body odour, wine and a considerable amount of Barcelona's refuse, but there's a simple explanation for all that, which I'd be more than happy to offer you, had I the time. Unfortunately, I don't. Are you following me?'

She nodded vigorously, but didn't seem entirely convinced. I concluded she must be a spoilt child who had been cosseted far too much.

'There's just one thing I'd really like you to understand,' I went on, trying to ignore the butler's shouts outside for me to open up at once: 'my freedom and that of my poor sister depend on the success of my investigation. This may not mean a lot to you, especially on the eve of your wedding to a rich and handsome young man, as your neighbours' maids have told me – and permit me to add, an extremely lucky

man too, to judge by the little I've seen of what he'll soon be
getting his hands on. May I, by the way, congratulate you and
wish you everlasting happiness. But as I was saying ... '

'The police are on their way!' I heard the butler shout.
'Come out with your hands up and nothing will happen to
you!'

'... as I was saying, I need to solve a case, and for that I
require your collaboration, Señorita Isabel.'

'What do you want from me?' asked the young woman,
her voice choking with sobs.

'You were a pupil at the San Gervasio school run by
the Lazarist nuns, weren't you? I know you were, because
I've seen your photo in the April 1971 edition of *Roses for
Mary*.'

'Yes, it's true, I did go there.'

'More than that, you were a boarder there, weren't you?
Until the fifth year. You were a good, hard-working pupil,
and the nuns adored you. But then one night you disappeared.'

'I don't know what you're talking about.'

'One night you mysteriously disappeared from the dormitory. You passed through several locked doors, crossed the
garden without the guard-dogs realising it, climbed over a
high railing or wall, and vanished into the unknown.'

'You're off your head,' she protested.

'You vanished into thin air. The Barcelona police couldn't
find you anywhere, then two days later you retraced your
steps and returned to the dormitory as if nothing whatsoever
had taken place. You told the Mother Superior you didn't

remember a thing, but I'm not so sure. It's impossible for you not to remember having achieved such notable feats twice in succession, or what you did and where you were during those two days when you were no longer in the land of the living. For the love of God, tell me what happened: by doing so, not only will you save a young woman from an uncertain future, but you will bring about the reintegration into society of a poor wretch whose only wish is to win the respect of his fellows and to have a decent shower.'

There was the sound of running feet in the corridor, then of somebody hammering on the door: the police had arrived. I implored the young woman:

'Please, Señorita Isabel!'

'I've no idea what you're talking about. I swear by all that's holy I haven't the faintest idea.'

Her voice rang with a desperate sincerity, but even if she had said this rolling about with laughter I would have had to take her word for it, as by now the door hinges seemed about to give way, and I could see a policeman's truncheon already smashing through the upper panel. I therefore did no more than offer my excuses for having burst in on her, and threw myself headfirst out of the window, just as the white-gloved hand of the first representative of the law was reaching out to grab me.

I fell onto the bonnet of one of the parked Seats. Apart from tearing the seat of my trousers, thereby adding to the general climate of eroticism characteristic of this day and age, when our Spanish starlets seem intent on showing off the faded glories of what were once their firm and appetising charms, I did myself no great harm. The policeman pursuing me obviously decided the wages he was being paid were not sufficient to compensate for the risks of plunging after me. Instead he contented himself with firing off his machine gun at the Seat, which I had already left well behind me. Its engine, bodywork, and windows were soon as full of holes as a Gruyère cheese. I should perhaps state here that I am well aware Gruyère cheese is not full of holes, they are in another sort whose name I forget for the moment, but that I am using this figure of speech simply because it is common in Spain to refer to any surface with holes in it as being like the former cheese – that is, Gruyère. I should also add that I was rather disappointed that the machine-gunned car did not burst into flames like they always do on TV, although I am fully conscious of the huge divide between reality and fantasy, and that art and life do not always coincide.

As I was saying, I leapt down from the car, cleared the hedge and sprinted off down the street, using my head as a battering ram to force a way through the curious onlookers attracted by the noise and shooting. I was fortunate that the police decided a priori that they were up against a probable rapist and so behaved with the disdain customary in such cases, rather than a terrorist, which would have led them to immediately surround the whole neighbourhood and employ all the latest technology in an effort to discover my whereabouts.

When I felt no longer at risk, I considered my situation: the interview with Isabel Peraplana could only be judged a total failure, and the dangers it had created out of all proportion to any benefit obtained. Yet I didn't feel completely downhearted, as I still had a trick up my sleeve – none other than Mercedes Negrer, whose existence until only a few hours earlier everyone had been so keen to cover up, for what seemed to me like weighty reasons.

9

A TRIP TO THE COUNTRY

There were ten Negrers in the phone book. I've always wondered why the authorities allow such a proliferation of names, as this detracts considerably from their usefulness and can only serve to create confusion among the public. What would our efficient postal service do if twenty places were called Segovia, for example? How would they collect the fines if lots of cars had the same licence plate number? What gastronomic pleasure would there be if every item on a menu was called Scotch broth?

This did not, however, seem an appropriate occasion for suggesting administrative reforms, and therefore I concentrated my efforts on a task I feared would prove laborious in the extreme. And so it proved. Fortune, which until then had smiled on me, now proved elusive, with the result that I had to make nine awkward calls until finally a female voice, which to my ears sounded slurred with drink, admitted that yes, she was Mercedes Negrer.

'It's a pleasure to talk to you,' I said, in my most urbane

voice. 'This is Spanish television, from our studios in Prado del Rey. Rodrigo Sugrañes, head of production, at your service. Would you be so kind as to allow us a few moments of your precious time? Yes? Of course you will. Let me explain: we are coordinating a new current affairs programme that we believe fits ideally into the spirit of the times. We are going to call it Youth and Democracy. We are therefore interested in interviewing the new generations born in the 1950s who will shortly be voting for the first time ... well, you get the picture. According to our information, you were born more or less in – no, don't tell me ...' I did a quick mental calculation – she was fourteen six years ago, so 1977 less twenty ... 'in 1957, isn't that right?'

'No, it's not,' the voice replied. 'I was born in ... well, that doesn't matter. It's my daughter you want to talk to.'

'Oh, what a silly mistake, Señora, but how was I to know you weren't your own daughter? You have such a youthful voice, such a delightful sing-song quality to it.... Could you please ask your daughter to come to the phone?'

At this there was a hesitation I was at pains to understand.

'No ... my daughter isn't here.'

'Do you have any idea when she might be back?'

'She doesn't live here.'

'Would you be so kind then as to give me the address where she does live?'

Further hesitation. Did the family suffer so terribly from having a wayward daughter?

'I'm afraid I cannot reveal my daughter's whereabouts, Señor Sugrañes. I'm really sorry.'

'Are you really going to refuse to collaborate with Spanish Television, which every night reaches into all of our great country's living-rooms?'

'I was told not to ....'

'Señora Negrer, listen to me: I have no idea who told you that, but I can assure you I'm not speaking on my own behalf, but on behalf of those millions of viewers who tune in to our programmes day after day. And on a confidential note, I should also say that the Minister of Information and Tourism, if such is still the title of that august governmental institution, has expressed great personal interest in our pilot programme!'

I was afraid she would hang up. I could hear her rapid breathing, and imagined her heaving bosom, with perhaps a trickle of sweat running down the centre of her cleavage. I had to control myself to drive away my fantasies. Then she spoke:

'My daughter, little Mercedes, is still in Pobla de l'Escorpí. Perhaps if, as you say, the minister is personally interested, he could intercede on her behalf with ... the relevant authority to bring her painful exile to an end.'

I hadn't the slightest idea what she was talking about, but had got the information I was after, and that was the main thing.

'Don't you worry, Señora: the TV can work miracles. A thousand thanks, and we'll be in touch again soon. We're on air!'

I left the phone box, which stank of dog piss, and looked at the time on the octagonal clock in the window of a corset shop: half past six. I went back into the phone box, called information, asked for the number of Spanish Railways, called them about forty times and by pure chance found someone to talk to. The last train for Pobla de l'Escorpí left in twenty minutes from the suburban station. I hailed a taxi and promised the driver a juicy tip if he got me there in time. We travelled half the way on the pavement, but he managed to reach the station two minutes before the train was due to depart. I took advantage of a red light to jump out of the taxi and lose myself in the rows of traffic. Unable to leave his cab to chase after me, the taxi-driver made do with cursing me with all his might. By the time I arrived in the grimy entrance hall it was departure time, and I wasted another minute checking which platform the train was leaving from. I sprinted there, only to find that it was still being made up, an expression commonly used in railway parlance, but one which I have never understood. Spanish Railways' proverbial lack of punctuality had come to my rescue yet again.

Both the platform and the entire station were in pandemonium. It was the season for that huge and lucrative influx of foreign tourists who year after year insist on coming to our country in search of our caressing sun, our crowded beaches, and the cheap delights of our everyday fare, consisting largely of watery gazpacho, suspect meatballs and thin slices of melon. Many of the confused tourists were trying in vain to translate into their own languages the garbled messages they could hear over the loudspeakers. Thanks to all the confusion, I managed to steal from a small child a brown travel-card that would allow me to travel legally. Later, on board the train, I saw his mother give him a clout round the ear after the conductor had asked for their tickets. I felt a bit bad about this, but consoled myself with the thought that this would teach him a valuable lesson for the future.

Night had fallen by the time our train left behind the last houses of the city and made its way through the dusty countryside. Although it was full and many passengers had to stand in the narrow corridor, nobody came to sit beside me, obviously because by now the smell from my armpits was overpowering. I decided to use their squeamishness to my own advantage, and, stretching out to my full length on the seat, I soon fell asleep. My dreams, in which the libidinous sociologist Ilsa featured prominently, soon took on a decidedly erotic tone, and climaxed in an uncontrollable ejaculation, to the great delight of all the children in the compartment, who had been following my body's strange jerks and protuberances with great scientific curiosity.

Two hours later, the train drew up at an old brick station blackened by a century of soot and neglect. All along the platform were lined up metal containers about a metre high, on the side of which was inscribed 'Mamasa Milk Products, Pobla de l'Escorpí'. I got off the train, as this was my destination.

A rocky, forbidding path wound its way up from the station to the village. I set off, uneasy at the silence broken only by the rustle of trees and the occasional sudden animal noise. The sky was full of stars.

The village appeared deserted. In the bar-restaurant Can Soretes I was told I would be sure to find Mercedes Negrer up at the school. As he said the word, Señor Soretes (I guessed this must be the owner himself) rolled up his eyes, clicked his tongue and brought his hairy hand down to a part of his huge body obscured by the bar counter. I left him doubled over and made my way to the school building, in one of whose tiny windows I could see a pale yellow glow. When I peered inside, I saw a classroom in which a young woman was sitting on her own marking a pile of papers on the teacher's desk. She had very short black hair, but I couldn't see her features. I tapped gently on the glass, and she gave a start. I pressed my face against the window pane and tried to smile, although the glass made this rather difficult, in order to reassure the teacher (I guessed this must be her) and Mercedes Negrer, who in fact was the person fulfilling that role.

When she took off her glasses and came towards the window, I immediately recognised her. Unlike her friend Isabel Peraplana, Mercedes Negrer had changed a lot, not so much as a result of the natural biological development of her anatomy, but because the expression in her eyes and the hard line of her mouth were very different from those that had stared out at me from the shiny pages of *Roses for Mary* a few hours earlier. I could not help but notice that her features were small, symmetrical and delicate; her legs, stuffed into a tight pair of black jeans, were long and apparently well shaped; her waist was narrow and her mammaries, straining against a ribbed woollen jersey, looked perky and abundant. I imagined she must be one of those women who had burnt her bra, a move of which I thoroughly approve.

The person answering the above description raised the sash window a couple of inches and asked who I was and what I wanted.

'My name would mean nothing to you,' I said, trying to push my lips closer to the opening. 'What I want is to talk to you. Please don't shut the window before you've heard what I have to say. Look, I've put my little finger on the sill. If you close the window now, you'll be responsible for any damage to my brittle bones. I know your name is Mercedes Negrer. It was your mother, that delightful woman, who gave me your address, something which, as a mother, she would not have done if she had not been certain that my intentions were entirely honourable. I have come here from Barcelona expressly to discuss something with you. I'm not going to do you any harm. Please.'

My pleading voice and sincere expression must have been convincing, because she opened the window a few more inches.

'Go on,' she said.

'What I have to tell you is confidential and might take some time. Couldn't we speak in a more relaxed atmosphere? At least let me come in and sit at one of the desks. I've never actually been in a classroom, since my studies were somewhat cursory, to say the least.'

Mercedes Negrer thought this over for a few seconds, during which time I succeeded in not staring even once at her inviting tits.

'We could go to my place,' she said eventually, to my surprise and delight. 'It's quiet there and I could offer you a glass of wine if you like.'

'How about a glass of Pepsi-Cola instead?' I ventured to suggest.

'I don't have anything like that in my fridge,' she replied with an unnecessary chortle, 'but if the bar is still open, they might be able to sell us a bottle.'

'It was open a minute ago,' I informed her, 'but I don't mean to cause you any trouble.'

'It's no trouble. I was already fed up with all this marking,' she said out loud, while she stuffed the papers she had been reading into the desk drawer, put her glasses directly in a cloth bag which she slung over her shoulder, and then switched off the classroom lights. 'Before, when I was at school, teaching was completely different. The kids had a great time with all the naive eroticism of the holy scriptures and the derringdo stories of our great imperial past. Now it's all about group theories, linguistic nonsense, depressing and highly improbable sex education.'

'So we lived better under Franco?' I suggested, remembering the phrase used by the saintly gardener.

'Any time in the past was better,' she said gaily, opening her mouth and the window at the same time, and sticking a leg out. 'Help me climb down, will you? I thought I was thinner than I am, and bought these jeans two sizes too small for me.'

I offered her my hand.

'No, not like that! Grab me by the waist. Come on, don't

be scared, I'm not going to break. I've been manhandled before. Are you shy, repressed or simply stupid?'

With that, she fell into my arms. I let her go as quickly as I could, and turned to look at the moon shining brightly over my shoulder so as to hide the obvious hard-on my brief contact with her had produced. The thought that our proximity must have allowed her to get a good whiff of my offensive smell soon brought me back down to earth. While all this was going on, Mercedes Negrer had closed the window and pointed out the route we were to take, namely in the direction of the bar-restaurant from where I had recently come. As we walked along, she said she was almost pleased to see me because, as I could tell, the village was not exactly a hive of emotions, and all this solitude was grating on her nerves. For the moment, I did not wish to ask her what had been the cause of her exile, or what kept her in a place she so obviously detested. I was aware that the answer to these questions was the reason for my being there, and was therefore to be broached with caution.

To my great delight, the bar was still open. The impulsive owner was busy wiping down the bar with a grimy cloth and one of those aerosols that tear great holes in the upper atmosphere. He gave Mercedes the Pepsi-Cola she asked for, all the time staring shamelessly at her womanly charms.

'What do I owe you?' asked the schoolteacher.

'A kiss from those cherry-red lips, sweetheart,' the barman said.

Undeterred by this rude remark, Mercedes took a cloth purse out of her bag, and laid a 500-peseta note on the counter. The barman put it in the till and gave her the change.

'When are you going to give me what we both know is right, Mercedes my love?' insisted the lustful innkeeper.

'The day I'm as desperate as your poor wife,' Mercedes retorted, already on her way to the door.

I realised I ought to make my presence felt so, once we were out in the street, I asked Mercedes if she would like me to go back into the bar and teach the foul-mouthed oaf a lesson.

'No, don't bother,' she said, although there was some doubt in her voice. 'He's one of those who says what he doesn't think. Most people do the opposite, and that's far worse.'

'Well anyway,' I said, 'I don't want to put you to any expense. Here, take your 500 pesetas back.'

'Not a bit of it. Keep your money.'

'It's not mine. The money's yours. I stole it from the till while that loudmouth was sounding off.'

'That's a good one!' laughed Mercedes, restored to her old cheery self. She put the note in her trouser pocket and for the first time looked at me with an air of respect.

'Are you sure,' I said, 'that my going to your place will not set people in the village talking?'

Still smiling, she looked me up and down.

'With all due respect, I don't think that's likely. Besides, I've already got a bad reputation here, and I couldn't give a shit.'

'I'm sorry about that.'

'You should be more sorry that what they say doesn't correspond to reality. As the nuns at my school used to say, the opportunities to offend God are not exactly legion in a backwater like this. Now that everyone is so liberated, the local girls have woken up and are more than ready for it. My problem is nobody trusts me. When they expanded the milk factory they brought in some Senegalese to work. Illegally, of course. They paid them shit and fired them the moment they started to wiggle their black bottoms.'

Living as she did far from the city and consequently from the latest linguistic fashions, Mercedes' saucy comments were not always politically correct. 'I thought I might be able to oil my machine with them, and while I was at it confirm the truth or otherwise of certain cultural myths. But I didn't even try. For their sake, of course. The villagers would have strung them up if they had so much as suspected something like that was going on.'

'Not you?'

'Not me what?'

'They wouldn't have lynched you?'

'No, not me. For a start, I'm not black, as you will be able to tell when we reach the next lamp-post. And then again, they've got used to me. At first they didn't know what to make of me. Then someone called me a nymphomaniac and that seemed to satisfy their intellectual curiosity. The magical power of language.'

'Yet they're happy enough to have you teaching their children,' I said.

'They don't have much choice. If it had been down to them, they'd have thrown me out long ago. But they can't.'

'Because you've been officially appointed by the Ministry of Education?'

'No. I'm not even qualified. But this village depends completely on the milk factory. Mamasa, it's called, I don't know if you saw the churns at the station. You did? Well, that's the explanation. Mamasa wants me to stay, so here I'll be until the end of time.'

'Who owns Mamasa?' I asked.

'Peraplana,' she replied, confirming what I had already suspected. The shadow of a doubt clouded her beautiful, astigmatic eyes. 'Did he send you?' she asked faintly.

'No, he didn't. I'm on your side, believe me.'

She fell silent, and I thought I wouldn't be able to get anything more out of her, but finally she said: 'I believe you,' with such conviction I guessed she was desperate to find someone she could confide in. Too bad, I thought. If only things were different ...

We reached the door of a large, ancient stone house that stood alone at the far end of a silent street. The back of this mansion gave directly onto the fields. A stream was babbling in the distance, while the moon lit a distant range of imposing mountains. Mercedes Negrer opened the door with a huge, rusty key of obvious priapic symbolism and invited me in. The house was sparsely furnished with items of rustic furniture. The walls of the tiny living-room she showed me into were covered with shelves filled with books. There were more piles of books on the table with a brazier, and on the cane chairs. In one corner stood a TV set covered in dust.

'Have you had supper?' she asked.

'Yes, thank you,' I said, although I could feel hunger knotting my stomach like a garrotte.

'Don't lie.'

'I haven't had a bite to eat in two days,' I confessed.

'It's always better to be honest. I can make you fried eggs, and I think there's a bit of ham left. I've also got cheese, fruit and milk. The bread's from the day before yesterday, but when it's toasted and with some oil and garlic on it, it'll do. I've also got some packet soup somewhere, and a tin of peaches. Oh, and there's some turrón left over from Christmas, though that must be hard as a brick by now. You sit and drink your Pepsi while I prepare everything. And don't go rummaging about among my papers, because you won't find anything.'

With that she left the room in what seemed to me like unwonted haste.

Left alone with my drink, I collapsed into an armchair. I took a few sips and, overcome with fatigue from all that had happened in the previous days and intensely moved not only by the expectations that the talk with my hostess had aroused in me, but above all by the tone of motherly concern with which she had spoken, I was on the verge of bursting into uncontrollable tears. But I resisted like a real man.

10

THE MURDEROUS TEACHER'S TALE

I had done justice to the scrumptious supper, and was nibbling at the turrón, which despite being stale tasted heavenly to me, when the clock on the wall struck eleven, as that was the time. Mercedes Negrer, who was sitting cross-legged on the mat, despite there being a wide variety of empty chairs in the house, surveyed me with an impish curiosity. With an abstemiousness typical of the well fed, all she had eaten were a few slices of cheese, a raw carrot and two apples. Once she had finished, she asked if I had a joint on me, to which I had to say no, because that was the truth, although I would have said the same even if I had had what she was asking for, because I wanted her to have a clear mind for the subtle questioning I intended to put her through. During the meal, as they say often happens when a storm is brewing, there had been strict silence – that is, if by silence we mean the lack of any verbal communication, because the sounds of my chewing, swallowing and belching had echoed through the house's cavernous stone walls. Once all that had quietened down, I gathered my thoughts and said:

'Even though until this moment all I have done is take advantage of your boundless generosity – for which I will be eternally grateful, as a lack of gratitude is not one of my many and weighty faults, although I should state in my defence that I am not entirely responsible for some of them – I now hope to be able to dispel the uncertainty surrounding my visit with a brief account of what led up to it and its precise purpose. It so happens I am investigating a small matter on which much depends. As I said, I am a man who means no harm, although I have not always been so: sadly, I have known both sides of the crucible, if that metaphor is correct, which I sincerely doubt, as I have no idea what the word "crucible" means. My straying from the straight and narrow led me to prison and other places I prefer not to mention, in order not to create a worse impression than the one my appearance already causes.'

'Stop a minute, linnet,' said Mercedes.

'But I haven't finished,' I said.

'There's no need,' she replied. 'I knew why you had come as soon as I saw you. Let's stop beating about the bush. What do you want to know?'

'About something that happened six years ago. You were fourteen then.'

'Fifteen. I missed a year with scarlet fever.'

'Alright, fifteen,' I conceded. 'Why did they expel you from the San Gervasio school run by the Lazarist nuns?'

'Because of lack of application and distaste for study.'

THE MURDEROUS TEACHER'S TALE

She had replied in great haste. I pointed to the book-shelves all around us. She got the message.

'Okay. In fact, it was for misbehaving. I was a rebellious teenager.'

I remembered that the saintly gardener had called her a little devil, although in fact this was the term he had used for most of the girls.

'You behaved so badly the usual punishments were not enough?' I asked.

'I don't know if you've ever read Simone de Beauvoir, but at that age girls change. Some of them accept the transition without fuss. I wasn't one of them. It's something that has been widely studied by psychiatrists, but in those days nuns were no experts in psychology. They preferred to think I was possessed by the devil.'

'You can't have been the first one.'

'No, and I wasn't the first to be expelled from a girl's school either.'

'Was Isabel Peraplana possessed by the devil as well?'

My question was met with a longer silence. Thanks to the lengthy psychiatric treatment I had received in the asylum, I knew this meant something, but I could not for the life of me remember what.

'Isabelita was a model student,' Mercedes said finally, her voice drained of all emotion.

'If that was so, why did they expel her?'

'You'll have to ask her.'

'I already have.'

'And her answer did not satisfy you.'

'There was no answer. She said she didn't remember a thing.'

'I believe her,' Mercedes added, with a strange smile.

'I thought she was being sincere too. But there must be something else. Something everybody knows, but is keeping quiet about.'

'They, or us, must have their reasons – if you count me as one of them. Why are you so keen to find out what happened? Are you interested in educational reform?'

'Six years ago, Isabel Peraplana disappeared from the boarding-school in unexplained circumstances, and reappeared equally mysteriously. This was apparently the reason for her being expelled from the school, as also happened to you, who were her best friend and consequently in all probability her confidante. While not wishing to jump to any conclusions, it seems legitimate to believe that both expulsions were related, and were closely connected to Isabelita's temporary disappearance. This of course is all water under the bridge, and is of no importance to me personally. But a few days ago – I am not sure exactly how many, because I've already lost count – another girl disappeared. The police have offered me my freedom if I find her, and that *is* important to me. You might say you couldn't give a damn about my freedom, to which I would have no reply, because that's life. But I can at least try. If I were ever guided by them, I would appeal to your love of truth, justice and other absolute values, but when it's a matter of principle I am incapable of lying. If I did, I would not be the useless wretch I have been all my life. I am not trying to coerce you or make promises, because I know I cannot honestly do either, and to do so would be little short of ridiculous, if not completely ridiculous. I'm begging for your help because that's all I can do, and because you are my last chance. Only if you take pity on me can I successfully conclude my search. That's all I have to say.'

'I'm sorry,' she replied, frowning as she stared at me, and breathing heavily. 'I make it a rule never to submit to emotional blackmail. It's not on. It's half past eleven now. The last train leaves at midnight. If you leave straightaway, you'll have plenty of time to catch it. I'll give you the money for the ticket, if that's alright with you.'

'Receiving money is always alright with me,' I replied, 'but it's not half past eleven, it's half past midnight. I saw at the station what time the last train was, and in anticipation of your reaction, put the clock back an hour while you were in the kitchen. I'm sorry to repay your hospitality with such a mean trick, but as I told you, this is really important to me. Forgive me.'

A few anxious moments followed, during which I was afraid she might hit me on the head with some object or other and kick me out. Then I noticed the same childish gleam of admiration in her eyes as when I had given her back the 500 pesetas in the bar: I sighed to myself, as I knew she wasn't going to punish me. If I had only remembered that in spite of her bravado little Mercedes was only twenty years old, I would probably not have worried so much to begin with.

'I hate you,' was all she said.

If my emotional experiences had at the time gone beyond the four filthy sluts who had left gaping holes in the wilderness of my heart, then at that moment I would have been possessed by a different and far more rational fear. But the chapter on pure passions was missing from the book of life that the years had beaten into me, and so I paid little attention to what seemed to me an entirely justified rebuke, or to the quivering her plaintive voice produced in my insides, which I in my stupidity took merely to be the consequence of the way I had just finished stuffing my face.

'Why don't we carry on where we left off?' I said. 'Why did they expel you from the school?'

'For killing a guy.'

'I beg your pardon?'

'Didn't you say you wanted direct answers?'

'Tell me what happened.'

'As you know, Isabel Peraplana and I were friends. She was the good girl; I was the bad influence. On top of that, she was the slow one, whereas I was sharp; she was naive, I knew it all. Her parents were rich; mine weren't. They had made enormous sacrifices to send me to that school. Obviously they weren't just doing it for me: it was their way of climbing the social ladder, unconsciously of course. I suppose I also shared their pretensions: I lived in the shadow of the Peraplana family, spending my holidays with them, being ferried around in their cars. They gave me clothes and stuff like that – the same old story.'

'Actually, it's the first time in my life I've heard it,' I said, trying to accommodate the image of an adolescent Mercedes to my feeble knowledge of opulence. Somehow the sight of her more than opulent bosom kept getting in the way.

'As you may well imagine,' she went on, 'this situation left a profound narcissistic wound in me, which naturally enough I found almost impossible to rationalise at that stage of my development. What I mean to say is that my ego must have been traumatised.'

'Please, let's just stick to the facts.'

'I can't remember how it all started. At some point when I wasn't around, Isabel Peraplana must have met a guy. I've no idea what can have been going through her spoilt brat's mind, what she saw in him or what deep-seated instincts he stirred up in her, for heaven knows what ends. The fact is that, as the saying goes, he seduced her.'

'He ****her?'

'I didn't say that,' Mercedes interjected. 'I was talking about romantic seduction. I'm only guessing.'

'Why are you only guessing? Didn't she tell you anything?'

'Why should she?'

'You were her best friend.'

'That sort of thing never gets told to best friends, sweetheart. Be that as it may, one night Isabel sneaked out of school to be with him.'

'Did she tell you what she was going to do?'

'No.'

'So how do you know she sneaked out of school to meet him?'

'Because of what happened later. Don't keep interrupting

me. As I was saying, Isabel sneaked out of school to be with him, but I'd already noticed the change in her attitude and was on the lookout. I caught her leaving and followed without her realising. No, don't interrupt me. When I reached their rendezvous, which took me a lot of hard work, I stumbled upon a terrible scene. I'll spare you the details. Perhaps the same scene would have appeared normal to me nowadays. But then I was still very young, and Spain was Africa beyond the Pyrenees. As I've already said, I felt I owed Isabel Peraplana a lot for everything she and her family had done for me. Possibly I thought I had the chance to make up for things my social position made impossible otherwise. Without even thinking, I picked up a knife and plunged it into the bastard's back. He died on the spot. The two of us had no idea what to do with the body. Isabel was hysterical. She called her father, who came at once and took charge of the situation. Worried by Isabel's disappearance, the nuns had already called the police. Señor Peraplana talked to someone called Flores, from the vice squad ... '

'No, from Criminal Investigation.'

'They're all the same. Anyway, the cops were very sympathetic. Isabel and I were minors. That meant we would be sent to reform school, and have our lives cut short. The police decided to consider the crime as self-defence. Isabel was taken out of school by her parents. I think they sent her to Switzerland, as rich people used to do in those days. I was sent here. The milk factory, which Peraplana owns, gave me money to live on. After a while, I persuaded them to let me pay my own way and do something useful. That was how I became the schoolteacher. The rest is irrelevant.'

'What did your parents say about all this?'

'What could they say? Not a thing. It was either accept what Peraplana was offering or go to reform school.'

'Do they come to visit you?'

'At Christmas and Easter. I can put up with that.'

'Where did you get all these books from?'

'At first my mother used to send them, but all she ever bought were the Planeta prizewinners, and you know what they're like. In the end I got in touch with a bookseller in Barcelona: he sends me catalogues and then the books I order.'

'What would happen if you returned to Barcelona?'

'I don't know and I don't want to know. The statute of limitations doesn't apply for another fourteen years, I believe.'

'Why can't Peraplana protect you just as well in Barcelona, Madrid, or anywhere else for that matter?'

'His protection only works because I'm so far away from everything, like someone dead and buried. In a small, enclosed village. And then there's the advantage of the milk factory.'

The clock struck twelve.

'One last question. Did the knife have a wooden or metal handle?'

'What does that matter?'

'I'm just interested, that's all.'

'For God's sake, that's enough questions. It's one in the morning. Let's go to sleep.'

'Yes, we can go to sleep, but it's not one o'clock. What I said earlier about the clock wasn't true: I made it up so I didn't have to leave. Once again, I'm sorry.'

'It's not important,' she repeated, without explaining whether she was talking about the time or the knife. 'You can sleep in my parents' room. The one they stay in whenever they come, I mean. The sheets may be a bit damp, but they're clean. I'll lend you a blanket, because it gets very cold in the early morning.'

'Can I have a shower before I go to bed?'

'No, the water is cut off from ten o'clock. It comes back on at seven in the morning. You'll just have to be patient.'

We went up a well-worn staircase and Mercedes showed me in to a large room that had a sloping ceiling with worm-eaten beams and bare stone walls. In the centre of the room was a four-poster bed with a mosquito net. She got a brown blanket that smelled strongly of mothballs out of the wardrobe. She showed me where the light switch was, and wished me sweet dreams before she withdrew, shutting the door behind her. I heard her steps disappearing down the corridor, another door open and close, and a bolt being drawn. I was exhausted. Without removing my clothes, I lay on the bed, switched off the light, and fell fast asleep, trying to find a plausible explanation for the pack of lies this strange woman had been telling me.

II

THE ENCHANTED CRYPT

A noise woke me. I didn't know where I was or what I was doing there: in the grip of fear, I could scarcely think. I groped instinctively for the light switch dangling from the frame of the four-poster, but still found myself in complete darkness. Either there was no electricity, or I had gone blind. I was covered in a cold sweat, as if I'd been taking a shower from the inside out. As always when I'm in a panic, I was overwhelmed by a desire to relieve myself. I listened as hard as I could, and heard footsteps in the corridor. The events of the previous night still filled my mind, but began to take on a new and ominous meaning: my supper had been poisoned, the conversation was a stratagem designed to lull me into a sense of false security that would make me easy prey, my bedroom was a mousetrap filled with elaborate torture devices. Now it was time for the final blow – a hammer, a dagger, then my body cut into pieces, the burial of my sad remains in the shade of the most hidden weeping willows beside the babbling brook, worms eating me up, oblivion, the black hole of non-existence. Who had conceived the plan to do away with me? Who had laid the trap I was caught in like a small, defenceless furry beast? Whose hand would carry out the sacrifice? Would it be Mercedes Negrer herself? The lecherous Pepsi-Cola man? The over-endowed Senegalese? Milkmen from the factory? I had to try to stay calm. To avoid being carried away by fears not as yet justified, not to allow my suspicions to block the means of communication, as Dr Sugrañes himself had so often told me in therapy. Your fellow man is good, I said to myself, nobody hates you, there's absolutely no reason for anyone to chop you up into little pieces, you haven't done anything to arouse the anger of anyone around you, even though they might seem to have it in for you. Stay calm. There's an explanation for everything, something that happened to you in childhood, or something that could be the projection of your own obsessions. Stay calm. In a few moments it'll all become clear, and you'll be able to laugh at your childish fears. You've been having psychiatric treatment for five years now, your mind is no longer a tiny boat adrift on the stormy sea of your fantasies, as when you were such a fool that you used to believe phobias were those silent and particularly deadly farts rude people let fly in crowded public transport. Agoraphobia, fear of open spaces. Claustrophobia, the fear of enclosed spaces, such as crypts or anthills. Calm, stay calm.

Reassuring myself with these comforting thoughts, I tried to climb out of bed. As I did so, what felt like a cold, heavy spider's web fell on top of me, pinioning me to the sheets. I could distinctly hear the doorknob turning, the creak of hinges, and then the sound of padded feet crossing the room, the heavy breathing of someone about to commit the foulest of crimes. This was enough for me to give in completely to fear: I wet myself, and started calling out in a low keening voice for my mother, in the vain hope that she might hear me in the great beyond and come to meet me on the threshold of the kingdom of the shades: I've always been nervous about visiting strange places. All this was going through my mind when I heard a voice beside me:

'Are you asleep?' I recognised it as coming from Mercedes Negrer, but when I tried to answer, all that emerged from my throat was a low groan that gradually swelled into a cry of alarm. I felt a hand on my back:

'What are you doing tangled up in the mosquito net?'

'I can't see,' I managed to gasp. 'I think I've gone blind.'

'Don't be silly. There's been a power cut. I've brought a candlestick, but I can't find any matches. My father always keeps a spare box in the bedside table so he can have a smoke when he wakes up, even though the doctor has forbidden it.'

I heard a drawer being opened close by my head, then a pair of hands rummaging inside it. There were the sounds of scraping and flaring, then a flickering flame which after it had been applied to a candle, gave off a dim light which allowed me to make out, through the mosquito net, the calm face of Mercedes Negrer, blinking rapidly. She was wearing a tartan flannel shirt which had once belonged to a man much bigger than her, from whose folds (those of the shirt) appeared her long, slender thighs. As she leaned over to disentangle me from the net, I saw beneath the shirt a pair of blue knickers whose flimsy material gave me a glimpse of a dark, unruly triangle, while at the rear I saw the outline of a pair of buttocks clenched as tightly as a fist at a workers' demonstration. Not all of the shirt buttons were done up, and in the dark recesses appeared velvety white shapes that gave off a warm, bittersweet aroma.

'I heard you talking in your sleep,' she said, then added somewhat illogically: 'I couldn't sleep either. Have you peed yourself?'

'I ate too much last night,' I said by way of excuse, blushing with shame.

'Don't worry, it happens to all of us. Do you want to go back to sleep, or shall we talk?'

'I'd prefer to talk, if you promise not to tell me any more lies.'

She gave a sad laugh.

'What I gave you was the official version. I never found it very convincing. How did you see through it?'

'The whole thing was completely implausible: for example, the idea that a terrified young girl could instantly kill a man by stabbing him in the back. I've never killed anyone, but I do know a bit about violence. From the front, it's possible, from the back, never.'

She sat on the edge of the bed, while I curled up on the pillow, with my back against the creaking wooden headboard. She raised her knees until she could rest her chin on them, and grasped her ankles. Personally, I found her idea of a comfortable position rather odd.

'The background is the same,' she began. 'The poor but bright girl on one side, the rich, rather dim one on the other. There's also the trauma ...'

'What happened on the night Isabel disappeared?'

'We used to sleep in the school dormitory. Our beds were next to each other. I had insomnia, which I now put down to the pressures of adolescence, but in those days attributed to anything but that. I could hear Isabel muttering in her dreams, and began silently to survey her radiant features, her golden, flowing hair, the perspiration pearling her forehead, the vague outlines of her recumbent body – does that sound too literary?'

I made no reply. I didn't want to say anything that might interrupt the flow of her thoughts. I know that no one is more inclined to beat about the bush than a person about to make a confession, so I resolved to be patient.

'After a while, Isabel got out of bed,' she went on. 'I realised she was still asleep, and thought she must be a sleep-walker. She went down the passageway between the rows of beds and headed straight for the door. I got up too and followed her – I was afraid she might bump into something and hurt herself. The dormitory door was always locked, but to my surprise I saw it open wide. Everything was dark: all I could see was a shadow on the far side of the door, in the corridor leading from the dormitory to the bathrooms.'

'Was it a man or a woman?'

'A man, if trousers are a way of defining gender. I already told you, everything was in darkness.'

'Go on.'

'Led by the shadowy figure which had opened the door, Isabel walked to the bathroom. There the shadow told her to stop, while he came back to lock the dormitory door again. By that time I had managed to slip out too, and was hiding round a corner, determined to continue the adventure to the end.'

'A question: was the dormitory door locked or bolted?'

'Locked. At least it was then.'

'Who kept the key?'

'The nuns, of course. As far as I remember, the matron had one, and the Mother Superior another. But I don't think it would have been hard to have a copy made. The regime at the school may have been strict, but we girls were quite timid, and so they probably didn't have to take too many precautions. Don't confuse a school with a prison.'

'Just one more question: what happened if a girl had an urgent need for the toilet in the night?'

'There was a lavatory and a wash-basin at the far end of the dormitory. Instead of a door it had a cretonne curtain, so that no one could shut themselves in and do naughty things.

'I'll go on. The bathrooms were deserted. Like Isabel, I was barefoot, and could feel the damp chill of the floor tiles on my feet. For some reason, that made me stare at the feet of my friend's mysterious guide: I could see he was wearing canvas slippers with a rubber sole. We used to call them "Wambas" because that was the commonest trade-mark. In those days they were cheap and lasted a long time – not like now, they're rubbish.

'At the far end of the bathrooms was another door. This led to a staircase that took you down to the chapel ante-chamber. When we had finished our ablutions, we girls used to line up there while matron inspected us. It goes without saying that at that time of night, the antechamber and the staircase were as deserted as the bathrooms. Isabel's mysterious guide lit the way with a torch. I had no problem following them from a distance, because my years at the school meant I knew the way by heart and could have followed it blindfold.

'I arrived at the chapel just in time to see them disappear behind the high altar, the one dedicated to the Virgin. For a while, I waited for them to reappear, because I knew there was no door behind the altar. When there was no sign of them, I tiptoed forward. They had vanished! I soon deduced they must have got out through some secret passageway, and started to search for it, trying hard not to give in to the superstitious fear that was gripping me. After several minutes of intensive searching by the pale light of the moon filter-ing in through the stained-glass windows, I saw there were four stones in the apse floor which, to judge by their Latin inscriptions and the skulls engraved in them, I thought must contain the mortal remains of four blessed souls. Curiously, one of the slabs didn't have any dust on it, and there were no signs of rust on the heavy ring set into the stone between the skull's cheery jaw and the inscription *Hic jacet v.h.h. Haec olim meminisse jubavit*. Screwing up my courage, I got hold of the ring and pulled as hard as I could. The slab gave way, and after repeated efforts I managed to pull it to one side. Below me stretched a dark staircase. Trembling with fear, I climbed down. At the foot of the stairs was a gloomy tunnel: I groped my way along until a side opening indicated another passage cutting across it. I didn't know what to do, but followed this new passageway, thinking I could always retrace my steps. A short time later, when a third passage crossed the one I was in, my blood ran cold: I realised I was in a labyrinth, on my own and in darkness, and that unless I found my way out quickly I could be breathing my last down there. Fear must have clouded my mind, because when I tried to get back to the stairs up to the chapel, I took a wrong turning. I crept from tunnel to tunnel, but couldn't find the stairway. I cursed my own foolhardiness, and was overcome with the darkest forebodings. I suppose I started crying. After a while, I set off again, thinking that I might find my way by chance if nothing else. I'd lost all notion of time or how far I had gone.'

'You didn't think of shouting for help?' I asked.

'Yes, of course I did. I shouted at the top of my lungs, but the walls were thick, and all I heard was a mocking echo. I stumbled on and on, until, when I was almost at the end of my tether, at the end of the passageway I saw a dim glow. The wind was howling, and I could smell a sweet smell in the air, a mixture of incense and wilted flowers. I advanced slowly towards the light, and had almost reached it when what seemed like a gigantic spectral figure loomed up in front of me. After all I had been through, this was too much: I fainted. Soon afterwards, I thought I had come round, but that cannot have been the case, because in front of me I saw a huge fly, about two metres tall and with a body to match. It was staring at me with its horrible eyes and seemed to want to connect its repulsive proboscis to my neck. I tried to cry out, but no sound emerged. I passed out again. This time, when I came to I was in a domed room dimly lit by the green light I have already mentioned. I felt the touch of a hand on my cheek, and hair was tickling my forehead. Thinking it must be the giant fly crawling over me, I tried again to scream, but immediately realised it was Isabel herself, whose blonde hair was brushing against me. Before I could even demand an explanation, Isabel put her hand over my mouth and whispered in my ear:

"I knew I could count on you. Your courage and loyalty will find their just reward."

'Then she withdrew her hand from my mouth and instead brought her hot, moist lips down on mine, while at the same time her body, which seemed to be floating in mid-air, settled on top of me. Through the flimsy veil of her nightdress I could sense the wild beating of her heart and the burning desire of her adorable form. Why hide the savage pleasure that took hold of me at that moment? We melted in a passionate embrace which lasted until my trembling hands and hungry mouth sought out ...'

'Whoa there!' I protested, somewhat taken aback by the direction her narrative was taking. 'I wasn't expecting anything like this.'

'Oh come on, sweetheart,' she said impatiently, as if annoyed at my interruption, 'don't be so narrow-minded. It's quite likely there was more than a mere schoolgirl friendship between me and Isabel. At that age, and in a boarding school, Sapphic tendencies are quite common. If you've ever seen her, you'll know that Isabel's body is angelic to say the least. Of course, she may not be so beautiful these days, because I haven't seen her since then. In those days at least, she was a smasher.'

This description, which years of sexual freedom had already rendered obsolete, brought a smile to my face. Mercedes misunderstood:

'Don't think I'm some sort of covert lesbian,' she protested. 'If I were, I'd say so. Everything I'm telling you about happened years ago. We were adolescents, fluttering around in the ambiguous light of our erotic dawn. My current preference for men is beyond all doubt. Just ask in the village if you don't believe me.'

'Alright, alright,' I said. 'Please, go on with your story.'

'As I was saying, I was busy enjoying myself in this way,' Mercedes took up the thread, 'when I noticed my fingers were stained with blood. I immediately saw it came from Isabel's body. When I asked her what it was, she said nothing, but took me by the hand and helped me up from the floor. She led me to a table at the far end of the crypt. On it lay a handsome young man, wearing the same Wambas I had seen in the dark bathroom. To all appearances, he was stone dead: he lay without moving, and a dagger was sticking out of his chest near the heart. Overcome with horror, I turned to Isabel to ask what had happened. She shrugged and replied:

"Are we going to argue over a little thing like that when we were having such fun? I had to do it."

"Why? Was he going too far?"

"No," replied Isabel with that spoilt little girl's pout she always put on when somebody tried to reprimand her: "It's because I'm the queen bee."

'In this of course she was not entirely mistaken, at least on a symbolic level, even though it is not scientifically proven that queen bees destroy the workers once they have been impregnated. There is of course the case of the female praying mantis, and that of some species of hymenoptera in Central America, where the female reproductive organs secrete a substance ...'

Once again, I had to interrupt Mercedes, as she was obviously keen to show off the knowledge she had in all kinds of areas. I asked her to get back to what had taken place in the crypt once they had discovered the stiff.

'I didn't know what to do. I was completely confused, and Isabel didn't seem to be in any state to offer help. I realised I had to do something to get my friend out of there before someone found us and she spent the rest of her life in jail. I calculated that in the world outside, day must have dawned, and that we had precious little time if we wanted to get back to the dormitory. From a practical point of view, I was not too concerned about the body, because it was unlikely the nuns would discover the passage down to the crypt. Even if they did, there was no way they could connect the murder with Isabel, providing we managed to return to the dormitory before the morning wake-up bell. The main problem was how to find my way through a labyrinth whose secret I did not know.'

'I was turning all this over in my mind when I heard a crashing sound behind me, as though something had smashed to pieces. I turned just in time to catch Isabel, who was about to fall to the floor. She was as pale as wax.

"What's wrong?" I asked her, terrified. "What was that noise?"

"My poor glass heart has broken," was her only reply.

'With that, she collapsed lifeless in my arms. The wind was howling round the crypt again, and I felt I could do no more. A stifled buzz told me the fly was still nearby. I crouched down to protect Isabel. We both fell to the floor. For the third time, I lost consciousness.

'I was awakened by the dormitory bell. I was in my bed, and a girl from the third form who was always sucking up to the nuns was shaking me.'

"Hurry up," she said, "or you'll be late for inspection. How many black marks have you had this month?"

"Two," I replied mechanically.

'Three black marks meant an unsatisfactory report; three bad reports and you got a verbal warning; two warnings led to a written report, three written reports and your parents were called in.

"I don't have any," boasted the toadie from the third year.

'A term with no black marks meant you got an award for hard work; if you had two awards in one year, you were given a Saint Joseph sash; if you won three sashes during your time at school, you were given the title of ... but perhaps all this is not so relevant to my story.

'In any case, I felt as though I was waking up from a terrible nightmare. My first impulse was to look across at Isabel's bed: it was unmade and empty. I thought she must have beaten me to the bathroom. I was wrong. When we had the morning inspection, her absence was noted. They questioned us for hours: I stayed quiet. At mid-morning that fellow Flores turned up, from the vice squad ...'

'I've already told you about that!'

'He questioned us all half-heartedly, then left again,' Mercedes went on. Like all people who think they know everything, she never listened when anyone tried to put them right. 'I didn't say a word to him either. That night I was so exhausted I slept like a log, even though my nightmares prevented it from doing me much good. I woke up the next morning when the bell went, and when I saw Isabel getting up from the bed opposite thought I must be going mad. All the noise the other girls were making prevented me from asking her what was going on, although neither her manner nor her appearance seemed to indicate any great change in her. She was as distant and insipid as ever. Again, I thought it must all have been a bad dream, and had almost convinced myself of this when matron appeared and took me off to the Mother Superior's office. Half-dead with fright, I went in and saw that my parents, Inspector Flores and Isabel's father, Señor Peraplana, were there with her. My mother was sobbing uncontrollably; my father was staring down at his boots like a man crushed by a sense of shame. I was told to sit down, someone shut the door, and the inspector began:

"The night before last there took place in this institution – which from the mere fact of being so, deserves all our respect – a crime for which our penal code offers a very precise definition (the same one, it should be said, as that offered by the dictionary of the Spanish Royal Academy). As a person who utterly repudiates violence (for which reason I joined the police force) I feel disturbed and distressed, and were it not for the meagre pittance I earn, would immediately pack my bags and head for Germany. Do you know what I am referring to, my girl?"

'I didn't know what to say, so I burst into tears. The Mother Superior was reciting the rosary; my father was patting my mother on the shoulder in a vain attempt to comfort her. The inspector reached into his trench-coat pocket and pulled out a bundle. With a flourish, he unwrapped this and revealed the bloody dagger I had seen protruding from the dead man's body in the crypt. He asked me if I had ever seen the murder weapon before. I said I had. Where? Sticking out of a man's chest, I said. At this, he delved into his bottomless coat pockets again and pulled out a pair of old Wambas. Did I recognise them? Again, I said I did. He told me to empty out my uniform pockets. To my astonishment, when I did so, together with a pencil sharpener, a rather grubby handkerchief, two rubber hair bands and a crib for the works of Lope de Vega, there appeared a duplicate of the dormitory key. I understood I was being framed for the murder Isabel had committed, and that my only way out was literally to pin it on her. Of course, I was emotionally incapable of doing such a thing. Besides, telling the truth would have meant also revealing the exact circumstances in which I had found her. I knew that if Isabel and myself were not to be ruined, none of the events of that night should get out. And yet, would I be able to make the ultimate sacrifice, even if it meant the gas chamber?'

'We don't have the gas chamber in Spain,' I noted. 'In fact, there are a lot of Barcelona suburbs which don't have any gas at all.'

'Do you mind not interrupting me?' said Mercedes, plainly annoyed at this unscripted diversion from the drama she was acting out for my benefit.

'"The punishment laid down in our legislation for this kind of crime," the inspector elaborated, "is the most serious imaginable. However ..." Here the inspector paused: "However, taking into account your tender age, and the troubled mental state that afflicts women at certain stages in their lives, as well as the intercession of the kind Mother here" – he jerked his thumb in the direction of the Mother Superior, with what seemed to me a certain lack of respect – "I am prepared not to proceed in the manner that my position as a servant of the people would normally require. By this I mean that in legal terms, there will be no official report or charges. We will avoid a trial in which the details, interviews, depositions, provisional and definitive sentences would only be extremely painful and somewhat saucy. In return, naturally, certain measures will have to be taken. Your parents, here present, have already accepted them. You should thank Señor Peraplana, also present, for the arrangements made. He has agreed to do this out of the affection his daughter feels for you, which he considers recip-rocated by yourself. Also for further reasons, which he has not seen fit to divulge, and which I couldn't give a damn about."

'The arrangements the inspector was referring to were nothing less than my exile here, which, given the alternative, I was happy to accept. So I came to this village, and here I am. I spent the first three years in an old couple's house, reading and getting fat. The milk factory gave them money each month for my board and lodging. After a lengthy strug-gle, I got them to agree I should be more independent. I appointed myself the village schoolteacher when there was a vacancy which, for obvious reasons, nobody wanted to fill. I rented this place. I don't live badly. The memory of what happened has faded. Sometimes I wish my fate had been different, but I don't wallow in self-pity. The air out here is healthy, and I have lots of time on my hands. As for my other needs, I told you yesterday I do what I can, which sometimes is not a lot, and at others is more than enough.'

Mercedes said no more, and the ensuing silence was bro-ken only by the crowing of a cock heralding a new dawn. I felt around me and was pleased to find the sheets were no longer wet. I was thirsty and tired, and my head was spin-ning. I would have given the world for a Pepsi.

'What are you thinking about?' she asked, with a strange edge to her voice.

'Nothing,' I replied like an idiot. 'What about you?'

'About how odd life is. I've been keeping my secret for six years, and now all of a sudden I spill it out to a foul-smelling lunatic whose name I don't even know.'

12

A PERSONAL INTERLUDE:

WHAT I WAS THINKING

'It's truly curious,' I said, 'how memory is the last survivor of the shipwreck of our existence. How the past deposits stalactites in the empty cave of our slender achievements. How the first slight breeze of nostalgia can blow down the walls of our certainties. I was born in a time which I a posteriori judge to have been a sad one. But I'm not making any special plea: it may well be that every childhood is bitter. The passage of time was my only playmate, and each night brought with it a sad goodbye. Of those days I remember that I gleefully threw time overboard, in the hope that the balloon would rise into the skies and take me to a brighter future. A crazy dream: we will always be what we have always been.

'My father was a good, hard-working man who supported his family making enemas from old tins previously containing a fuel in great demand at that time for use in a device called the Petromax lamp, now happily supplanted by our abundant electricity supply. Some Swiss pharmaceutical laboratories set up in Spain as part of a development project ruined his business. Father had mixed fortunes throughout his life: he emerged from the fratricidal crusade of 36–39 not only wounded, but an ex-combatant and ex-prisoner of both sides, a position that brought him a lot of bureaucratic headaches but neither reward nor punishment. He stubbornly refused the few chances offered him by fate, but blindly accepted every fantastic scheme the devil could tempt him with. We never had any money, and he squandered what few savings we might have had by betting on the crab lice races held every Saturday night in the local bar. Towards my sister and me he displayed a possessive indifference: he expressed his affection in very subtle ways, so subtle it took us years to realise that that's what it had been. His irritation, on the other hand, was unmistakable; it never needed any interpretation.

'With my mother, everything was different. She had a true mother's love for us all: absolute and catastrophic. She always believed I would be somebody, while at the same time she was always aware I was a good-for-nothing. From the outset she made it plain she forgave whatever betrayal I was bound, sooner or later, to make her suffer. Thanks to the scandal over disabled children and the Eucharistic congress – you probably don't remember that, you must have been only a child, or perhaps had not even been born – she ended up in the women's prison at Montjuich. My father saw all this as a plot hatched with the sole intention of annoying him. My sister and I used to visit my mother on Sundays, and smuggle her the morphine without which she would have been unable to bear her imprisonment so cheerfully. She had always been a very active woman, for many years working as a skivvy, or as casual domestic help as it's properly called. She never lasted long in any employment because of her uncontrollable urge to steal all the most visible objects from the houses she worked in, including wall clocks, armchairs, and, on one occasion, a child. Despite this, she was very rarely unemployed, as the demand in those days, and still I believe today, far outstripped supply, and lazy people seem willing to put up with anything if it allows them to do nothing.

'The fact that our mother was in jail and our father had abandoned us meant my sister and I had to fend for ourselves from a very early age. My poor sister was never very bright, so I was the one who had to look after her. I showed her how to make money, and even found her first clients, despite the fact that she was nine and I was only four. At eleven, fed up with constantly being pursued by social services, having somehow contracted venereal disease, and wishing not to waste the talent which in my ignorance I thought I possessed, I decided to become a novice at Veruela ...'

The sound of a distant whistle cut short my outpourings and brought me back to reality.

'Is that a train whistle?' I asked.

'The milk train,' said Mercedes, 'why?'

'I have to go. There's nothing I would like better than to be able to continue our little chat,' I said, with the only sincere words I had spoken since the days when I swore to my sister's clients that I had a hot cherry-pie waiting just for them, 'but I have to leave as soon as possible. Thanks to you I have the key to the case that brought me here. All I need is a little extra information and the proof that my suspicions are correct. If everything goes according to plan, by tonight I will have confirmed your innocence, and within a few days you can be maid of honour at Isabel's wedding. And of course those who are guilty of all this shady business will be where they deserve to be, not that I have any idea where that is. Do you have faith in me?'

I was expecting her to utter a resounding 'Yes!' but instead Mercedes remained sullenly silent.

'What's the matter?' I asked.

'You didn't tell me Isabel was getting married.'

'There are lots of things I haven't told you, but by tomorrow I'll be back, and then nothing will ever interrupt us again.'

I presumed her silence was due to the natural shyness produced by intense emotion, and so, heart swollen with joy, I skipped my way back along the path to the railway station. There I managed to clamber on board the last wagon of a dilapidated freight train whose engine was already chugging along a valley at the foot of the mountains surrounding the village. In the early morning light, these hills appeared so green they looked like that precious stone whose name I always confuse with a well-known brand of bleach.

My wagon was full of fresh fish, and their salty smell led me to dream of other, happier climes and a life of shared delights. In the mad way that this kind of fantasy can produce,

I saw premonitions in the least little thing, the clear sky, the gentle breeze, the fish eyes, even in the name Mercedes, at once the patron saint of Barcelona and the epitome of Teutonic car-manufacturing. Even then, however, part of me resisted turning these fantasies into anything more concrete, because deep down I was afraid that once her name had been cleared, Mercedes might no longer want to have anything to do with me. Too much came between us. I even thought of giving up my investigation because, I told myself, as long as she was condemned to live in this exile and I was the only one who knew her secret, then I had her, so to speak, in the palm of my hand. But as I have already said in another part of this story, I am a new man now, and therefore I rejected the temptation, not without the fervent hope that for once a good deed would be rewarded in this world and not in the next, for which I felt neither love nor attraction.

The train-ride took forever. By now the sun was high in the sky, and the wagon was like an oven. The fish began to stink to high heaven. I kept throwing the most offensive specimens onto the tracks, but after I had completely emptied the boxes I discovered to my horror that the stench was still unrelenting, and had clung indelibly to my clothes and skin. I decided that all I could do was to be patient, so I lay down in a corner, and spent the rest of the journey devising plans, dreaming up projects, resolving enigmas and unmasking all the deceit and lies of which the woman for whom my heart was beating so fast had been the unsuspecting victim. None of this however prevented me from viewing my future with a certain degree of pessimism. Even if I did manage quickly and successfully to solve the case of the disappeared girl and to demonstrate Mercedes' innocence, there was still the small matter of the dead Swedish sailor, which the police seemed determined to pin on me. In the hypothetical event that this mystery could also be elucidated, I thought to myself, then what would become of me? With my police and asylum records, together with my complete lack of any profession, knowledge or skills, it would not be easy for me to find a well-paid job that could be the basis for a home and family. According to what I had heard, rents were sky-high, while the average shopping basket was soaring too. What was I to do? My daydreams were lost in a clammy mist.

It was well after noon by the time the train pulled into Barcelona-Terminó station. I jumped down from the wagon and hid under the wheels of the Madrid express, although soon afterwards I was forced to leave my hiding-place when an ear-splitting blast, in keeping with such a high-class mode of transport, warned me it was about to set off. Once outside in the street, I quickly ran to the place where sooner or later every investigator ends up, the Land Registry, situated in a peaceful, sunny office on Calle Diputación. I arrived a few minutes before it was closing. A hastily invented pretext soon permitted me to examine all the documents I said I required. The stench of rotten fish, on top of all the previous smells on my clothes and body, quickly drove away the few sleepy assistants wandering up and down the aisles, as well as the thrusting young men determinedly searching for plots of land with which to speculate. Within a few minutes I was free to undertake all the researches I needed, and it was not long before my suspicions were confirmed: the land now belonging to the Lazarist nuns had between 1958 and 1971 been owned by Don Manuel Peraplana, who sold it to the nuns for an exorbitant sum after having acquired it in 1958 for a fraction of the price from someone by the name of Vicenzo Hermafrodito Halfmann, born in Panama and by profession an antique dealer, resident in Barcelona since 1917, the year in which he in turn had purchased the land and had the mansion built. I was certain that this Panamanian must have constructed another house adjacent or close to the first one, and had for some reason or other connected the two properties by means of a secret tunnel which led from the fake tomb in the chapel apse. Peraplana had probably discovered the tunnel and used it for his own perverse ends. But why had he sold the mansion to the nuns in 1971 if he was still using the passageway? And where exactly did it lead? I tried to discover what other properties Peraplana or the aforementioned Halfmann owned in the area, but the registry showed the distribution of land rather than its owners, which meant I was out of luck. I therefore concluded I needed to speak directly to Peraplana, and so headed for his house once more, only too aware of the dangers awaiting me.

13

AN UNEXPECTED AND
REGRETTABLE ACCIDENT

When I reached the door of the Peraplana mansion I was faced with an unforeseen problem: a small crowd (however paradoxical that might seem) was gathered outside the garden hedge. Among the curious onlookers I recognised the maids I had wheedled information out of the day before, and so imagined that the wedding, which according to my calculations was due to take place in a few days' time, had for some reason or other been brought forward. I got my hands on a magazine at a nearby kiosk, hid my face behind it, and joined the group by the house. All the while, I was wondering how on earth I might manage to slip inside the limousine taking the bride and her father to the ceremony, if my idea about the required formalities for a wedding was correct. It seemed to me well nigh impossible, but was something I had to attempt if I did not want the newly married couple to leave on their honeymoon for Mallorca or wherever it is that the wealthy head on these occasions, which would have made my strenuous efforts even less likely to succeed.

We all continued to wait, and to while away the time I began to glance at the magazine. I rapidly came to the conclusion that in our day and age young people wrote about politics, art and society, whereas the older generation sought solace in the charms of the erotic. A fellow countrywoman of Ilsa's by the name of Birgitta, whose breasts seemed rather large considering her early stage of development, was running her hands over her body 'to discover the Orphic mysteries of her budding curves'. The crowd around me suddenly stirred, preventing me from reading what were undoubtedly the fantasies of a rutting pig. Raising my eyes and the corresponding portion of my head above the magazine, I saw the front door to the Peraplana mansion open, and two grey-uniformed policemen emerging. At first I was worried for myself, but soon realised they were not there on my account: they stood to attention on the steps as if expecting a procession to come out. I deduced that some local dignitary must be attending the wedding, and was just about to shout 'Long live the bride!' when I noticed that behind the policemen came a pair of ambulance men pushing a body on a bed which had what looked like bicycle wheels, as well as a nurse who was holding up a bottle filled with a maroon-coloured substance connected to the recumbent figure by means of a small tube. A doctor in a hospital gown and several other people were also escorting the trolley. One of them must have been Señor Peraplana, but as I had never seen him before, I could not swear to it. Whatever the liturgical changes introduced by the most recent Vatican Council, it was plain this was no wedding party. This was confirmed by the presence at upstairs windows of grieving women drying their tears with white calico handkerchiefs. A gasp went up from the gathered crowd, and the police cleared a way through for the stretcher towards a waiting ambulance. I asked a man standing on tiptoe next to me what exactly had happened.

'A tragedy,' he told me. 'It's the poor girl from the house. She committed suicide this morning. And just before her wedding day. We are as nothing, my dear friend.'

He seemed happy to talk, so I decided to inquire a little further.

'How do you know it was suicide? Cancer is no respecter of age.'

'I hung up my cassock to get married after ten years as a priest,' said the man. 'Between everything I heard in the confessional and all that I've learnt since, there's not much I don't know.'

He started to chortle at his own joke. So that he would not feel silly, I did the same. Then he put a sweaty hand on my shoulder while with the other he wiped away the tears from his eyes.

'I wouldn't want you to think I'm a miracle-worker or a clairvoyant. It was the boy from the Bou butcher's shop, who curiously enough is called the same, but with a "w" – Wou, heaven knows where he comes from – who told me what had happened. He was in the kitchen when the fuss started, delivering their meat. Are you interested in this sort of thing?'

I told him the news had affected me deeply.

'Life is like a leaf tossed here and there by the wind,' he said. 'Carpe diem, as the Romans used to say. Do you like women? I'm sorry, I don't mean to be nosey, but I saw you looking through that magazine. Believe me, all this nakedness is a commercial stunt designed to make money from our frustration. I've nothing against the pleasures of the flesh, what I can't stand are cheap substitutes. Real women of flesh and blood, and real coffee too, as we used to say in my younger days. I'm not trying to pretend to be better than I am; I have my weaknesses. Each time I read one of those magazines it drives me nuts.'

But I was no longer listening to his ranting. As I thought of poor little Isabel, whose charms I had been admiring only a few hours earlier, two big teardrops rolled down my cheek, and a trail of snot dripped from my nose. My unworthy tribute to our fleeting dreams, to the ephemeral nature of human beauty. However, this was no time for philosophising, because another idea had taken root in my brain. I started looking round me for a face I knew. Since I am not particularly tall, I had to jump up and down in a way that was rather ill-suited to the occasion, but I soon discovered the object of my search: a woman who was hiding her face beneath a black, broad-brimmed hat and dark sunglasses, as well as thick, garish make-up that thoroughly spoiled her delicate features. This vain attempt at disguise confirmed for me the very different criteria men and women have with regard to beauty. Women tend to think that attractiveness has to do with their eyes, lips, hair and other attributes situated to the north of their gullets, whereas the masculine gender, if I may so call them (apart from the occasional deviant) focus their interest on a completely different part of the female anatomy, and couldn't give a stuff about the rest. So, despite all Mercedes Negrer's efforts to go unnoticed, a mere glance at her incendiary bristols would have been enough to identify her a mile off.

Having thus espied her, I forced my way head down through the crowd to join her. When she saw me approaching, Mercedes tried without success to get away, since her struggles only encouraged those she was pushing against to try to get closer still. Thanks to this, I had soon grasped her by the arm and pulled her, despite her desperate struggles, to one side of the group of onlookers. I led her off smartly to somewhere quieter, and once we came to a halt, I said:

'What have you done, you wretched creature?'

She burst into tears, smearing the make-up she had applied all over her face.

'How did you get here before me?' I pressed her.

'I have a car,' she said, coughing and spluttering.

Knowing how little schoolteachers earn, I hadn't considered this possibility, but nor had I taken into account how generous the milk factory had been: what she received each month from them allowed her to spend her salary on extras.

'Why did you do it?' I insisted.

'I don't know. I can't find any logical explanation for what happened to me. I was quite calm after you left this morning. I started preparing my healthy breakfast when suddenly, as if attacked by a wild beast, all these years of frustration and rancour bore down on me. It might have been resentment at a life sacrificed for what I had thought was a noble cause. It might have been because I learned that Isabel was getting married ... I want to die. I'm scared stiff; I've no idea what will happen to me now. All those years for nothing ...'

'What exactly happened?'

'I got into my car and came here as fast as I could. I called Isabel from that phone box over there: she got the shock of her life when she heard me, because she thought I was study-ing abroad somewhere, the ninny. I said I had something important to tell her, and we agreed to meet in a nearby bar. I was convinced that if I saw her it would ease my tor-ment, but it only made it worse. I knew she would only talk nonsense, so I got in first and started insulting her: I said I had always known she was stupid, selfish, narrow-minded and two-faced. She didn't know what I was talking about, and thought I must be off my head. So I told her what had happened six years earlier in the boarding-school crypt, and said I saw her hands covered in blood, possibly the blood of her lover. I threatened to go public with the dreadful affair unless she immediately broke off her engagement. All I wanted to do was to get my anger off my chest, to wreak psychological revenge. But Isabel, who had probably never read Freud, took what I said literally. Of course, it may also have been that my story brought memories submerged in her subconscious back to the surface. Poor Isabel never had sufficient strength of character to confront the dark side of life. Faced with this crisis, her defences crumbled; she went home and committed suicide.'

'How do you know?'

'After our meeting I hung around outside the house. I felt rather sorry for what I had said. I saw how depressed she was when she went in. Soon afterwards, all hell broke loose. The doctor arrived, and the butler received him in a panic. Hidden behind the hedge, I could make out the words "suicide" and "poison".'

'Where on earth did you get that make-up and that outlandish gear?' I asked, more to take her mind off her despair than out of any real interest.

'I had them at home. Sometimes I used to dress up and look at myself in the bedroom mirror. I'm repressed. I've never been to bed with a guy. Men scare me. My so-called promiscuity is all a front for my lack of experience. I'm so ashamed of myself!'

'There, there,' I said in my best paternal manner, 'we can talk about that some other time. For now, there's a lot for us to clear up. If you do as I say, as I promised by tomorrow the case will be solved.'

'What's it to me if the case is solved?'

'To you, I'm not sure; but to me it means a lot. My sister's in jail, and my freedom, if not my neck, is on the line. I'm not going to give up now the finishing line is in sight. I'm ready to go on alone if need be, but you could help me a lot. You've committed a reckless and useless act: Isabel never killed anyone and never had a lover. The least you can do is help demonstrate her innocence. It's also the only way to make up at least partially for what you have done, unless, that is, you prefer to spend the rest of your days consumed with remorse. Then again, what other choice do you have? Now that Isabel is dead, there's absolutely no reason for Peraplana to go on having the milk factory keep you. Either you decide to take control of your destiny right now, or you'll end up ... well, like me, to look no further.'

My words seemed to comfort her, because she stopped crying and began to redo her make-up thanks to a small oblong case with a tiny mirror and a powder puff. I remembered that my sister used to put her make-up on with the corner of a floor-cloth, and sighed to think that even the most insignificant details only served, or serve, to underline social divisions.

'What do I have to do?' asked Mercedes submissively.

'Have you got your car nearby?'

'Yes, but the oil needs checking.'

'What about money?'

'I brought all my savings just in case I had to run away.'

'That shows this was premeditated, gorgeous. But we'll come to the charges against you all in good time. For now, let's pick up the car: on the way I'll tell you what I've found out and what my plan is.'

THE MYSTERIOUS DENTIST

It was time for dinner for those who could afford such luxuries, and once again the streets were half empty. It had begun to rain, so heavily that the drops bounced off the bonnet of Mercedes' car, a dilapidated 600 that was about to pass from the status of old crock to holy relic, in which we sat waiting for some sign of life from the Peraplana household. The bereaved family members had returned home an hour earlier. It would have been normal for them to spend the rest of the night mourning their loss; yet I suspected that something was about to happen, and my suspicions were soon confirmed.

First the butler appeared, sheltering beneath a stripy umbrella. He opened the gate as wide as it would go, then stepped to one side as powerful headlights pierced the darkness. A Seat, not the one that had been machine-gunned, but the other car, came roaring out of the drive. There was only one person inside. I nodded to Mercedes, and she prodded her old banger into what little life it could muster.

'Try to stay on his tail, even if it means you have to give up on the mental arithmetic the Highway Code requires in order to calculate the distance between you and the car in front,' I said.

We set off so close behind the Seat I was worried we were going to hit it. By law of course that would have been our fault, because the driver of the car behind is always held responsible, even if the other driver has caused the action by word or deed. In this way we reached Diagonal Avenue, where I took advantage of a red light to leap out of the car, after insisting to Mercedes:

'Don't let him get away. And for God's sake, put your glasses on. Nobody is going to see you, and they could help prevent a serious accident.'

She said she would, set her mouth in grim determination, and shot off in pursuit of the Seat. I hailed a taxi I had spotted, jumped in and told the driver:

'Follow those two cars. I'm from the secret police.'

'So am I,' he said. 'Which branch?'

'Drugs,' I improvised. 'How is the wage bargaining going?'

'Badly, as usual,' grumbled the bogus taxi driver. 'We'll see what happens at these elections. I'm going to vote Felipe González: what about you?'

'Whoever my bosses tell me to,' I said quickly, to avoid any further discussion which might give my game away.

We had gone round Calvo Sotelo Avenue and continued on down Diagonal. Just as I had thought, the driver of the Seat soon realised he was being followed, and suddenly turned off the wrong way down Calle Muntaner. Poor Mercedes was caught completely off-guard, and was almost hit by a bus as she valiantly tried to back up. I smiled to myself and told the taxi driver to follow the Seat. Confident he had shaken off his tail, the Seat driver slowed down, making it easy for us to keep up with him. Not only that, but I had managed to free myself from Mercedes for a while, without doing any further damage to her already almost non-existent self-esteem.

The Seat reached its destination, a corner house on Calle Granados. The car pulled up and the driver got out. He disappeared into the dark doorway, head sunk on his chest as though the rain would not be able to reach it there. The door opened and the Seat driver was swallowed up. I asked the driver to wait, but he said that was impossible.

'I have to go and patrol round Reventós' house, to see if I can unearth anything.'

I thanked him and wished him luck. He wouldn't take any money because I was a colleague, even though I was flush with all the notes Mercedes had given me before we split up. The undercover cop drove off, leaving me in the pouring rain. A hasty survey of the Seat offered few clues. The disc was in the name of an estate agency, so it was obviously some tax dodge. I hit the lock with a brick until it gave way, and searched the inside of the car. In the glove compartment all I found were the car documents, a badly folded road map, and a torch missing its batteries. The seats were plush velvet, but the driver also had a cane mat to avoid his backside getting too sweaty. From this I deduced it was Peraplana himself who usually drove the vehicle, and that therefore it was very likely he was the man who had just vanished inside the house. I made a mental note of the car's mileage, although I wasn't sure I would remember it: I find I am naturally more artistic than mathematical. The ashtray was littered with Marlboro cigarette butts. There was no trace of lipstick on any of them, but they betrayed the marks of a set of regular teeth, probably adult rather than milk. From the ash on the mat, it looked as though it was the driver who smoked. One of the filter tips was wet, and the automatic lighter was still warm. By now I was sure it was Peraplana himself in the house. In order to disguise my search as a robbery, I yanked out the radio and cassette player. I threw them both down the street drain, and for a few moments considered the possibility of hiding in the car boot to see where it was going, but immediately dismissed the idea as too dangerous. I was also more interested in what was going on in the house, and why Peraplana had come here while the earth was still fresh on his daughter's grave.

In a tapas bar across the way I ordered a Pepsi and shut myself in the phone booth with a handful of coins, making sure I could see the building opposite. I looked up the address in the phone book, and started to call all the inhabitants listed. When they answered, I said to each of them:

'Hi there, this is Cambio 16 magazine. We're doing a survey: what TV channel are you watching at this very moment?'

Everybody said they were watching Channel One, except

for some oddball who was tuned in to Channel Two. Only one number I rang answered curtly 'None,' and hung up.

'You took the bait, mate,' I said to myself, confirming the name of the person who had been so rude to our national press. Plutonio Sobobo Cuadrado, dentist.

Making sure I kept an eye on the building opposite, I drank the rest of the Pepsi. I had just stuck my tongue into the neck of the bottle to make sure I drained the last drop, when I saw two men emerging from the doorway across the street. They were carefully carrying a large bundle wrapped in a white sheet. A woman was watching them from the gloomy doorway, wringing her hands in despair. The size and shape of the bundle suggested it was a not very large person, in all probability a young girl. When the two men opened the car boot and pushed their bundle in, I was very glad I had changed my mind about hiding there. Then one of the men got behind the steering wheel, and the Seat set off. I would have liked to follow, but there was no taxi to be seen. I therefore turned my attention to the other man. He went back inside the doorway, exchanged a few animated words with the woman still wringing her hands, and then shut the wooden door. I paid for my drink, left the bar and stood watching the doorway in the teeming rain. I soon spotted what I was after, the details of which I will not go into here as they interest only locksmiths and burglars, and quickly went to look for a metal bar on a nearby building site. I used it to force open the door to the entrance hall, and once inside read the floor and number of the dentist's flat on the mailboxes: Second floor, Flat 1. There was a coffin-like lift, but I preferred to take the stairs so as to make no noise. The inside of the building matched its grey, heavy, vulgar and rather sad exterior: a typical block of flats in Ensanche. When I rang the dentist's bell, somebody immediately responded through the spyhole.

'Who's there?'

'Doctor, I'm in agony from a gumboil,' I said, puffing out my cheek.

'There's nothing wrong with you, it's out of hours, and anyway my surgery is in El Clot,' replied the dentist.

'Actually the truth is I'm a child psychiatrist,' I said, trying a different tack, 'and I'd like to talk to you about your daughter.'

'Get away from here at once, you lunatic.'

'If that's what you want, I'll leave, but I'll be back with the police,' I said, trying desperately to sound convincing.

'I'm the one who'll call the police if you don't go away right now.'

'Doctor,' I replied, less aggressively, 'You're caught up in something that's beyond your control. We need to have a frank talk about it.'

'I haven't the faintest idea what you mean.'

'Yes you do; otherwise you wouldn't be having a conversation like this, which no sane person would contemplate. I know all about your daughter, and however strange it may seem, I can help you out of the mess if you're willing to co-operate. I'm going to count to five: slowly, but I'll get there. If by the time I've finished you haven't opened this door, I will leave and you alone will be to blame for the consequences. One ... two ... three ...'

From behind the door panel I could hear a woman's faint voice:

'Open up, Pluto. He might really be able to help us.'

'Four ... and five. Good night to you both.'

At that, the door opened and in the doorway stood the figure I had seen earlier in the street. The woman was still wringing her hands behind her husband's back.

'Wait,' said the man. 'There's no harm in talking. Who are you, and what do you have to say to me?'

'We don't need the whole neighbourhood to know, do we, Doctor?' I said. 'Why don't you ask me in?'

The dentist stood to one side, and I stepped into a reception room dimly lit by a 40-watt bulb encased in a wrought-iron frame. The only furniture was a ceramic umbrella stand, a carved wooden coat-rack, and a hard wooden armchair. The wallpaper was patterned with a rural scene. On the inside of the door hung an enamelled plaque which read 'Bless This House'. The floor was covered with coloured octagonal tiles that were loose underfoot.

'Please come this way,' said the dentist, pointing to a dark, narrow passage that disappeared into the distance.

I set off, followed by the dentist and his wife. I felt a sudden qualm that I had not insisted we talk on neutral ground: I had no idea what awaited me at the far end of the corridor, and the capacity of dentists to inflict pain is well known.

15

THE DENTIST COMES CLEAN

My fears proved groundless. Halfway down the passage, the dentist pushed in front of me and politely switched on a light to reveal a small living-room, modestly but comfortably furnished. He invited me to sit in one of the armchairs, saying as he did so:

'We cannot offer you anything to drink as we would like, since both my wife and I are teetotallers. I can give you some medicinal chewing-gum a laboratory sent me as a sample. They claim it does wonders for gums.'

I declined the offer, waited for them both to be seated, and began:

'You may be wondering who I am and what I am doing prying into your affairs. All I can say is that the first of these questions is unimportant, and that I would find it hard to explain the second, beyond saying that in my opinion we're all in the same stew – although I can't even be sure about that until you have answered some questions I would like to put to you. A short while ago I saw you carrying a heavy bundle, which you placed in the boot of a car. Am I right?'

'Yes, you are.'

'Will you also admit that the bundle contained – or more exactly, was – a human being, presumably a girl, and, may I be so bold as to venture, in fact none other than your very own daughter?'

The dentist hesitated, so his wife took the lead:

'Yes, it was our girl, sir. You are quite right.'

I noticed that though she was somewhat broad in the beam, she was still worth looking at. There was an undefinable sadness in her eyes and in the taut line of her lips, and in general there was an air about her I could not quite place.

'And is it not also true to say,' I went on, remembering the elegant turns of phrase the prosecution counsel used whenever I had appeared in court and, I suspect, in all other cases as well, 'that the girl in the bundle, that is to say your very own daughter, was the same girl who disappeared two nights ago from the San Gervasio school run by the Lazarist nuns?'

'Keep quiet,' the dentist warned his wife. 'We don't have to answer him.'

'We've been found out, Pluto,' she said. She sounded relieved. 'I'm glad. We've never broken the law before. You look like a criminal, so you must agree with me it's no easy thing to silence your conscience.'

I nodded vigorously, and went on:

'In fact, the girl did not disappear from the school. Unbeknown to the nuns, she was taken out and brought here, where you hid her, despite putting on an act of being so distressed at her being kidnapped or running away. Isn't that so?'

'Yes, it's exactly as you say,' confessed the wife.

Which led directly to my next question:

'Why?'

Neither of them said a word.

'What was the reason for this ridiculous farce?' I insisted.

'He made us do it,' said the dentist's wife. Turning to her husband, who was glaring at her, she added:

'It's better if we come clean about everything. Are you from the police?' she asked, addressing me this time.

'No, Señora, far from it. Who is he? Peraplana?'

She shrugged. The dentist hid his face in his hands and burst into tears. Seeing a dentist weep so despairingly was strangely moving. I waited patiently for him to recover his composure. Once he was himself again, Cuadrado flung his arms wide as if he were about to beat his breast. Instead, he launched into a long speech:

'You, sir, who seem to be an observant and alert kind of person, will have noticed from the neighbourhood we live in, from the modest way we dress and live, and the way we automatically switch off the light whenever we leave a room, that we are part of the suffering middle classes. My wife and I are both of humble origin: for my part, I was only able to study thanks to scholarships and private classes offered to the faithful by the Jesuits. My wife's talents are limited to her culinary skills (not always in evidence) and her abilities as a seamstress, which enable her to alter summer dresses into housecoats she never wears. Even though we were married thirteen years ago, our meagre income has unfortunately only permitted us to have the one child, and seen us forced to use contraceptives, despite the fact that we are both practising Catholics, and this has robbed our sexual relations of all pleasure because we are so mortified with remorse. It goes without saying that from the moment of her conception, our little girl has been the centre of our lives. We have made untold sacrifices on her behalf, and have never called her to account for them – not explicitly at least. Fate, which has been against us in so many other regards, has rewarded us with a daughter full of good qualities, not the least of which is the love and devotion she professes for us.'

Perhaps in order to seek her support, the dentist turned towards his wife, but she sat with eyes closed and furrowed brow. She seemed to be far away, as though reflecting on the life she had led. Naturally, I didn't come to this conclusion merely from her withdrawn attitude, but from the way she reacted later on, which you will hear about all in good time.

'When our daughter reached school age,' the dentist went on, 'my wife and I had lengthy and often bitter discussions about where to send her. We both agreed this should be the best the city had to offer, but whereas my wife inclined towards a non-religious, progressive and expensive school, I was in favour of the kind of traditional religious education that has borne such wonderful fruit for Spain. I should add I don't think that all the changes so recently seen in our society will have a lasting effect. Sooner or later, the military will make sure things return to normal. In modern schools, it seems to me, anything goes: the male teachers brag about their irregular marital arrangements; the female ones don't wear any undergarments; at break-time sport is discouraged in favour of lustful activities; schools organise dances and excursions of more than one day; they show X-rated films. I don't know if, as they say, this prepares children to face the outside world. Perhaps it does inoculate them against danger: I prefer not to give my opinion. What was I talking about?'

'About the choice of your daughter's school,' I reminded him.

'Oh yes. As I was saying, we argued, and since she is a woman and I a man, she had to give way, as is only natural. The San Gervasio school run by the Lazarist nuns, which I finally chose, meant a double sacrifice for us. Not only were we separated from our little girl, as there were no exceptions to the rule of it taking only boarders, but we also had to pay fees which I can categorically state were, both relatively and absolutely, a heavy burden. However, the education she received was excellent, and so we never complained, although God knows we had little money to spare. And so the years rolled by.'

He waved his hands in the air as though conjuring up scenes from his dreary family saga. Seeing that nothing materialised in front of him, he went on:

'Everything was fine until I read an article in one of the free magazines I am sent about the advances the Germans are making in the field of orthodontics. I'll spare you the details: suffice it to say I became obsessed with the idea of buying an electric drill and mothballing the pedal one I had used until then, which, I must admit, was not always to my clients' satisfaction. I went to all the high-street banks, but they denied me the credit I was asking for, so I had to turn to other institutions that were rather more demanding in terms of the interest they charged. I signed promissory notes. I received the drill, but the instructions were in German. I tried it out on my patients, and lost several of them. The notes I signed came due astonishingly quickly, and I had to take out fresh loans to cover them. To cut a long story short: I was in it up to my neck. My religious beliefs and my responsibilities as father and husband meant I could not contemplate the coward's way out, suicide. All I had to look forward to was imprisonment and dishonour. The very idea that my wife should go out to work seemed repugnant to me. I'm not looking for excuses, I simply want you to understand my situation and to have some idea of how desperate I was.

'One morning an elegant, serious-looking gentleman turned up at my practice. I thought he must be serving a seizure notice or bringing a warrant for my arrest, but he was not a bailiff, as his appearance had led me to believe, but a financier who refused to identify himself but claimed to know all about my problems. He said he could help me. Hearing that, I tried to kiss his hand, but he raised it and left me sucking air. He asked if I had a daughter at the San Gervasio school. I said I did. He wanted to know if I was willing to do him a favour and could keep a secret. He gave me his word my girl would come to no harm. What could I do? I was, as they say, between a rock and a hard place. I agreed to do what he wanted. Two nights ago he brought our daughter home: she looked so pale I thought she might be dead, but the man said it was nothing, that he had simply had to give her a sedative as part of his plan. He gave me a box of capsules she was supposed to inhale every two hours. Thanks to my professional background, I realised they contained ether. I tried to go back on our deal, but the stranger silenced my protests with a sardonic laugh like the one I am going to imitate for you now: haw, haw.'

'"It's too late for regrets," he told me. "Not only do I have the IOUs you signed in my possession, which I will make public at the first sign of any backtracking, but your situation is now a matter for the courts. Neither you, your wife, or your daughter will escape facing charges unless you strictly follow my instructions."

'So we have spent the past two days, terrified and helpless, keeping our daughter drugged and just waiting for the force of the law to descend upon us. Tonight the same gentleman reappeared and ordered me to hand over the girl again. We wrapped her in a sheet and put her in the car boot, as you say you saw. That's all.'

He fell silent, and was once more racked with sobs. His wife stood up, walked across the living-room to the window, and stood staring at the mouldy geraniums out on their tiny balcony. When she spoke, it sounded as if her voice was coming all the way up from her stomach.

'Oh, Pluto,' she said, 'I curse the day I married you. You've always been ambitious without any drive, a tyrant with no nobility, a humourless fool. You've been vain in your dreams and a coward in reality. You've never given me anything I wanted, nor anything I didn't want, which I would have appreciated just as much. Of my endless capacity for suffering you have taken advantage solely of my submission. With you it is not passion I have missed, but tenderness; not love, but a sense of security. If I had not been so afraid of the miseries of solitude and penury, I would have already left you a thousand times. But this is the straw to break the camel's back. Find yourself a lawyer and we can start the process of separation.'

With that she sailed out of the room, oblivious to her arm-waving husband, who seemed to have been struck dumb. We heard her footsteps along the corridor; then a door slammed.

'She's shut herself in the bathroom,' the distraught dentist told me. 'She always does the same when she gets an attack of the hysterics.'

I always make it a rule not to get involved in other people's marital disputes, so I stood up to leave, but the dentist grabbed me with both hands and forced me to sit down again. There was the sound of a tap running.

'You're a man,' he said. 'You'll understand. That's how women are: you give them everything on a plate, and they complain. You give them their head, and they complain again. But we men are the ones who have all the responsibility, we're the ones who have to take the decisions. They are the ones who judge: if things work out, that's just fine and dandy; if not, you're there to be henpecked. Their mothers filled their heads with fantasies, so they all think they're Grace Kelly. But of course, you have no idea what I'm talking about. I can tell from your expression you couldn't give a damn. Looking at you, I can see you're one of those who gets everything for free. Your sort don't have any worries: you don't send your children to school or to the doctor; you don't have to buy them clothes and make sure they're fed: you send them out naked into the streets to fend for themselves. You don't care what cards fate deals you. You dress in rags, live crammed together like pigs, never go out of an evening and can't tell a sirloin steak from a squashed rat. Economic crises leave you untouched. As you have no expenses to meet, you can spend whatever you have on your vices; after all, who is going to hold you to account? And if you don't have enough, you go on strike and expect the state to save your bacon. Then you grow old and, not having saved a penny, throw yourselves into the arms of social security. And in the meantime, who are the ones bringing progress to Spain? Who are the ones paying taxes? Who is keeping the house in order? You say you don't know? Why, it's us, my good man, we dentists!'

I told him there was a lot of truth in what he was saying, said good night and got out of there as quickly as I could. It was late and I still had several loose ends to tie up. As I was walking down the corridor, I could hear the sound of water splashing from what I assumed was the bathroom.

Out in the street, taxis were conspicuous by their absence, and I knew I couldn't rely on public transport. I set off at a

THE MYSTERY OF THE ENCHANTED CRYPT

trot, and was soaked to the skin by the time I reached the bar in Calle Escuders where I had arranged to meet Mercedes. I found her surrounded by creatures of the night who were trying desperately to pick her up. Coming as she did from a decent, self-respecting village, the poor girl was obviously terrified by their shamelessness, but when she saw me come in she put on a show of amused bravado. One individual, whose open shirt-front gave a glimpse of a rug of hair and several tattoos, peered at me with bloodshot, challenging eyes.

'We could have met in a café,' Mercedes said accusingly.

'I couldn't think of one,' I replied.

'Is this your ponce, sweetheart?' said the man with the revealing cleavage.

'My fiancé,' retorted Mercedes.

'Well, I'm going to make Findus fish-fingers of him,' roared the braggart.

With that he picked up an empty wine bottle by the neck and smashed it against the marble counter. The pieces shattered in his hand, which began to bleed profusely.

'Shit!' he exclaimed. 'It always works in the movies.'

'Those are trick bottles,' I told him. 'Can I look at your hand? I'm an intern at the general hospital.'

As he showed me his bloody hand, I emptied a salt cellar on it. He howled with pain, and I hit him over the head with a bar stool. He fell to the floor. The barman asked us to leave as he didn't want any trouble. Once we were outside, Mercedes began to cry.

'I couldn't follow the car like you told me. He lost me. Then I got very scared.'

She was so upset I felt very tender towards her, and almost regretted getting her into all this.

'Don't you worry, Mercedes,' I told here. 'I'm here now, and everything will be fine. Where's your car?'

'It's badly parked on Calle del Carmen.'

'Let's go and find it then.'

We reached the car just as they were towing it away. It took a lot of arguing for the wardens to let us pay the fine and keep the vehicle. In return for the money we handed over, they gave us a carefully folded receipt and warned us not to read it until after they had gone. When we did, it read as follows: 'You are constant in your affection, but your reserve may give rise to misunderstandings. Wrap up warm.'

'I'm afraid we've been swindled,' I said to Mercedes.

16

THE CORRIDOR OF A HUNDRED DOORS

It was almost two in the morning by the time Mercedes succeeded in parking the 600 in a side street relatively close to the San Gervasio school. I slung all the gear we had bought that afternoon over my shoulder and we set off along the deserted streets. Thank goodness it had stopped raining.

'Remember what I told you,' I said to Mercedes. 'If there's no sign of life from me in two hours ...'

'I know, I call Inspector Flores. You've told me that a hundred times already. Do you think I'm stupid?'

'No, it's just I don't want to run any unnecessary risks,' I apologised. 'I don't know what I'm going to find in that damned crypt, but I do know that whoever's using it is capable of anything.'

'To start with,' said Mercedes, 'you're going to have to face the giant fly.'

'There's no such thing, silly. What you saw was someone wearing a gas mask. It seems these people are hooked on ether.'

'Shouldn't you take a canary with you?' Mercedes suggested.

'That's all I need,' I groaned.

We had come to a halt outside the spiked iron gate. The silence was total, and there was not a single light on in the school. I sighed: I was getting cold feet. Mercedes whispered in my ear:

'Be brave.'

I didn't like to mention it, but having to depend on her – from what little I knew, she had just committed a moral assassination, and the few other details she had seen fit to divulge – was precisely what worried me most.

'Wish me luck,' I said, as I'd heard them say in films.

'In case I never see you again,' said Mercedes, in a somewhat tactless manner, 'there's something I want you to know: when I told you this afternoon I was repressed, it was a lie. I've had countless lovers. I slept with all the Senegalese: men, women, children and camels. The whole tribe.'

I imagined that the danger must have overheated her imagination, so I said I believed every word. In the meantime, I had found what I was looking for: a pile of dog-shit, freshly made. I carefully picked it up off the pavement, making sure I did not disturb the original shape, then threw it through the bars of the gate into the school garden. The two mastiffs appeared in a matter of moments. They behaved exactly as I had expected, because I have observed that dogs, who are supposed to be intelligent creatures, like nothing better than to sniff at the excretions of their fellow canines. The mastiffs proved to be no exception to this sad rule. While they were having fun with this cheap gift that had fallen into their laps, Mercedes and I ran round the back of the building, where the garden wall was lower. I climbed onto her shoulders. Despite my slight build, she began to sway like a sailing boat in a storm, but I eventually managed to reach up to the top of the wall and to spread over it a blanket we had bought that afternoon. This enabled me to haul myself up without the shards of glass embedded in the top turning me into an ecce homo. I reached down and pulled up the rucksack Mercedes was holding up for me. Taking a quick look round, I saw the dogs were still nowhere to be seen. I took a succulent sausage bought in the Ninot market out of my bag: if the hounds reappeared, the idea was to distract them with this new gift from the gods. I jumped off the wall, the soft grass breaking my fall. Mercedes tugged on the other end of the blanket to remove all traces of my incursion into the school, but as she did so, something unexpected happened: a second blanket we did not even know existed fell out of the folds of the first one and landed right on top of me, leaving me looking exactly like a ghost. I stumbled over a protruding tree root, and fell in a heap. It was then I remembered that in the blanket shop I had seen a big sign telling all couples about to marry that if they bought one, they would be given a second identical blanket completely free, whether they wanted it or not. Since Mercedes and I had not behaved in any way that might give rise to this kind of conclusion about our relationship, I hadn't paid any attention to the offer.

Be that as it may, as I was saying, I was caught up in my struggle with the blanket when I heard threatening growls and could feel through the wool (if indeed that was what the blanket was made of) the wet muzzles of the two guard dogs, who in a spirit of great self-sacrifice had abandoned their sensual pleasures and come rushing to the spot where they had heard a crash. Fortunately for me, every brand-new blanket gives off a special and not exactly pleasant odour; this meant the mastiffs could not detect the presence of a human being beneath the cloth. Determined to use this unexpected turn of events to my advantage, I clasped the sausage firmly between my teeth (it seemed far too hard for the astronomical price I had paid for it) and started crawling on all fours across the lawn, trying to ensure that none of the extremities with which I am endowed poked out from under the covering. In this way, escorted by the dogs, who must have been racking their brains to decide what kind of creature this was, I reached the school wall. Now came the crucial moment: I had to emerge from my shelter and somehow get inside the building.

Carefully lifting one edge of the blanket, I threw the sausage away as far as I could. The dogs took off after it. Freed from their attentions, I returned to the vertical and closely examined the wall in front of me. To my horror I discovered it had no windows, creepers, or anything else that I might be able to climb. The hounds were racing back towards me, one of them triumphantly bearing the sausage in its jaws. In desperation, I threw the blanket over them both, trapping them underneath and thus reversing the roles that only moments before they and I had been playing in the great theatre of the world. I suppose they started biting each other or, shielded from prying eyes, engaged in libidinous pursuits – dogs are not backward when it comes to having a bit of fun. I meanwhile ran round the school as close to the wall as I could, until I found a tiny window left open because of the warm weather. I slid in with all the agility that panic provides.

I had no idea where I was, but the sound of snoring indicated I had landed in a cell where a nun was fast asleep. I took the torch we had also purchased that afternoon out of my rucksack, only to find when I tried to switch it on that I was holding the sausage, and that in my understandable nervousness, I had thrown the torch to the dogs. Trying to stay as far away as I could from the snores, I groped my way blindly until I came across a door. The doorknob turned easily, the door opened in front of me, and I was soon out in a corridor. I felt my way along it. Unfortunately, the corridor turned several times at right angles to the left, so that before long I was back where I had started. By now I had lost all idea of where I was or what time it was. I didn't want to try any of the doorknobs my hand blundered into, because I was worried they only led to other cells with sleeping nuns. Yet, rejecting the idea that there was no way out of the corridor, or that the nuns climbed in through the windows to sleep every night, I reasoned that one of the doors must connect with the rest of the building. But which one?

Sticking a finger up my nostril, something I find always helps me concentrate, I reflected on the peculiar idiosyncracy of religious orders and soon came up with the solution to my conundrum. I made my way all round the corridor yet again, feeling each doorknob as I went. I discovered to my joy that only one of them was locked. Thanks to a nail file I was also carrying in my bag, and the experience gained during my criminal career, I picked the lock and found myself at the foot of a staircase leading up to the first floor.

I soon reached a refectory where the tables were already set for breakfast. That reminded me I hadn't eaten a thing since supper the previous night. I sat at one of the benches and polished off the sausage, which despite being raw tasted heavenly. Suitably replenished, I set off to explore again. I will abbreviate my seemingly endless wanderings through the school by saying that, thanks to Mercedes' precise description, I finally found the door to the girls' dormitory. Once again, I picked the lock, and sneaked in stealthily so as not to wake any of its occupants. The dormitory was a vast rectangular room with two lines of beds along each side. On the left-hand side of each bed was a small table, and on the right stood a chair where the girls' uniforms lay neatly folded, with on top of them – oh disturbing vision! – each girl's pair of knickers. I did a quick calculation and came to the conclusion I was the only male among sixty-four little female angels at the height of puberty. All I had to do now was work out which of the sixty-four girls was the dentist's daughter, and the first stage of my plan would be successfully completed. You will doubtless be asking yourself, dear reader, how I was going to identify the girl in question, whom I had never laid eyes on. If this is the case, you will find the answer in my next chapter.

17

IN THE CRYPT

For the second time that night, though not in my life, I got down on all fours and began to crawl in between the beds, feeling the shoes lined up beneath them. They were all damp from the rain, except for one pair, the ones belonging to the dentist's daughter. Having thanks to this simple measure singled out the object of my search, I now had to put into action the second and most dangerous part of my plan. Out of my rucksack I took a handkerchief soaked in Purodor, a product usually to be found in the toilets of local cinemas. I used it to cover my nose and mouth, then tied it behind my head. I looked like a baddie in a Western movie. Then I got out an ether capsule that Mercedes had snitched from a pharmacy while I distracted the assistants by pretending I wanted a box of condoms but was too shy to ask. I sawed through the top of the capsule with the nail-file, and pushed it under the nostrils of the girl, where the ether evaporated. In less time than it takes to count to five, she sat up in bed, threw off her sheet and cover, and put her feet on the floor.

Gently taking her by the arm, I led her towards the door. She did not even seem to notice. I closed the door behind us, and we made our way through the bathroom, staircase, the antechamber and finally the chapel itself. Inside, we quickly reached the bogus tombstone with the inscription *V.H.H.* and the words *hinc illae lacrimae*. I left the girl standing next to a big wooden sideboard where liturgical objects were kept, and pulled as hard as I could on the ring protruding from the stone. The blasted slab didn't budge an inch, and I wondered how Mercedes, who six years earlier had been nothing more than a gawky adolescent, could have lifted it all on her own. I tugged and tugged, until finally the slab gave way. Pushing it to one side, I discovered I was staring down at a dark, foul-smelling hole. I stepped down, stumbled, and fell flat on my face. I found myself embracing a disgusting skeleton. Only just managing to stop myself crying out in terror, I clambered out of the hole as quickly as I could. I was trying hard to work out what had gone wrong, until suddenly the penny dropped and I cursed my stupidity. Silly me! I had been in such a hurry I had chosen the wrong tombstone, and had desecrated the one containing the mortal remains of *V.H.H.* If I had not been so completely ignorant of all foreign languages, I would have realised that the inscription engraved on the stone I had just lifted was not the same as the one Mercedes had mentioned. But as a result of my stupidity I had confused the two inscriptions, like the Swiss man I had once met, whose knowledge of Spanish was confined to the words 'bloody hell', which he repeated at every opportunity, convinced he was speaking our glorious imperial tongue and that anyone who heard him was bound to understand exactly what he wanted. When we had met, I sold him talcum powder as cocaine, which the presumptuous and obtuse man paid over the odds for and inhaled enthusiastically until he was off his head. Now here I was being equally obtuse. Always remember, dear reader, there but the grace of God ...

Once I had recovered from the shock, although my heart was still pounding, I used the handkerchief covering my respiratory organs to wipe the sweat from my brow. I then absent-mindedly put the handkerchief back in my rucksack – a momentary lapse which as you will soon see was to cost me dearly.

The genuine stone, as one might call it, was next to the one I had lifted. It gave way at the first pull, giving access to the steps Mercedes had described to me. I started down them, pushing the girl in front of me just in case there was a hidden ambush. It was completely dark in the tunnel, and I bitterly regretted the loss of my torch. As a precaution and possibly also out of nervousness, I gripped the girl's arm so tightly she started to call out in her dreams. While I admit my behaviour was none too considerate, I should like to re-mind anyone who objects that we were entering a labyrinth and that only this silly cataleptic girl I had succeeded in enlisting was capable of guiding me safely through the maze of tunnels. That was why I had kidnapped her; I was hardly down in this basement to be her private tutor. And I would say to anyone who thinks something else that the girl had a face like a suckling pig and was at that stage of development when there was nothing to be done with her beyond the realms of education. Of course, there will be others who claim that just because she had once, in a hypnotic state, found her way through the labyrinth didn't mean that she could repeat the procedure successfully a second time. To them I would respond that they were perfectly correct, since we had not taken a hundred steps before we were completely lost. We went on walking and walking, one tunnel leading to another, and then another, and the only logic behind the maze seemed to be in the twisted mind of whoever designed such an absurdity.

'I'm beginning to fear, gorgeous,' I said to the girl, even though I was well aware she could not hear me, 'that this is the end. I won't pretend I don't care, because I am fervently, some would say unjustifiably, attached to this carcass of mine, although there is some poetic justice in the fact that a cretin like me should end his days in this architectural allegory of my path through life. I am though truly sorry that you should have to share my fate without any reason. Such apparently is the destiny faced by some people, as your own father seemed to be suggesting to me only a few hours ago, and who am I to call into question the ways of the universe? Some little birds exist only to pollinate flowers, which other animals eat to produce milk. And there are people who see a lesson in all this chain of events. Perhaps there is one, I have no idea. As for me, poor soul, I have always tried to do it my way, without even trying to understand the mechanism of which I am perhaps only a tiny part, like the glob of spit they put on tyres in garages after they have inflated them. Then again, this philosophy, if it can be called that, has not been a great success. So here you have me, my child.'

This sad soliloquy, a resumé of my drifting course down the river of life, did not prevent me sensing that the rarefied, dusty air in the tunnel we were in was gradually becoming impregnated by a faint smell of haircream or aftershave lotion. I immediately suspected there might be a crook lying in wait for us. I paused to get the hammer I'd bought for defensive purposes out of my rucksack; to do this I had to let go of the girl. When I went to grab hold of her arm again, my fist closed on emptiness. Let me say in passing that I am aware that a gun would have been more useful than a hammer, but to buy one in a gun-shop would have led to all kinds of headaches over a licence, and the black market for weapons had become impossible now the spread of terrorism everywhere had sent prices sky-high.

At first I thought she must have got ahead of me, so I tried to hurry to catch her up, but found my legs getting heavier and heavier: it was becoming a real effort just to keep going. I felt a sudden pain in my stomach, which I put down to the sausage I had just guzzled, and felt dizzy in a not unpleasant way. I fell over, stood up again and carried on walking, endlessly, endlessly, until it seemed to me I had never done anything else in my entire life. All at once I saw a dim green glow in the distance, and thought I could hear a voice calling out to me:

'Hey, you, what are you waiting for?'

At this, although I would have been quite happy to sit down on the floor then and there, I made a determined effort to head towards the light, mainly because the voice urging me on belonged to Mercedes, and I thought she might need my help. I found it so hard to move I had to leave the hammer and my rucksack on the ground, and the only reason I didn't leave the few rags I still had on my back behind as well was because such a stupid idea never even occurred to me. All of a sudden the sound of a whistle wounded my ears, and as I tried to raise my hands to protect them, I realised I couldn't lift my arms.

'Come on, come on,' said Mercedes' voice.

All the while a voice inside me was saying: 'Idiot, don't be fooled: all this is a hallucination. The tunnel is filled with ether. Be careful: this is only a hallucination.'

'That's what they all say,' Mercedes cackled. 'But then you all behave as if it weren't, you pigs. Come over here and grab a handful, then we'll see if I'm simply the fruit of your imagination.'

Her figure, by now, clearly silhouetted against the greenish light of the crypt, stretched out inviting arms. They seemed barely to reach any further than the pair of celestial melons swinging between them.

'Only a mirage could have guessed at what my intentions are towards you, Mercedes.'

'What does that matter,' she replied, without defining exactly what she was referring to, 'so long as it helped you find your way again?'

Then a voice in the gloom behind me added: 'Although the deception isn't going to last very long, my little dove.'

When I tried to turn round to see who had uttered such a

threat, Mercedes got me in a bear-hug worthy of Bengoechea paralysing Tarrés during a wrestling match at the Iris Arena. It was impossible for me to defend myself, let alone procreate, as I almost demonstrated on the spot.

'Who goes there?' I asked, scared stiff.

At this, a muscular black man with oiled body and wearing a lamé loincloth emerged from his hiding place. Seeing I could not move, he came up to me, fondled my buttocks and said with cutting sarcasm:

'I'm the little boy from the jungles of Africa, like in the cocoa advert' he said, then added, snapping the elastic of his bodywrap against his oily skin: 'and I'm going to show you the many advantages of this matchless outfit.'

'I'm not gay,' I shouted, to make sure he got the message. 'Like everybody else, I've got my problems, but I'm not what you think. I have nothing against gayness, apart from the fact that I don't see why we can't use a proper Spanish word for it, especially when there are so many perfectly good synonyms in our own language. This phenomenon seems to me to indicate not only how our culture bows down to anything foreign, but also that we feel embarrassed to call a spade a spade, pardon my French.'

The black man however had taken a paperback out of his bulging loincloth, and was reading out a passage in a flat tone.

'Everyone has a certain amount of ambivalence latent in their personality,' he recited, before stuffing the book back between his legs. 'We all need to learn to accept this without pride or prejudice. As you yourself can see, for example, he said, pointing to the bulge in his loincloth, 'what is said about black people is entirely cultural. Forgive me for the play on words, but a love of paradox is inherent in all non-complex cultures.'

'Hallucination or not,' I said, struggling free with some regret from Mercedes' embrace, 'you're not going to submit me to any cheap and dubious psychoanalysis. I came here to solve a case, and that's what I intend to do, with or without your permission.'

So saying, I ran for the far end of the crypt, happy to make a quick rather than a glorious exit. As I sped along, I wondered what could have become of the poor dentist's daughter. I had a mental picture of her still wandering aimlessly through the tunnels of the labyrinth, but then all of a sudden I crashed into a hard, horizontal structure which brought me back to reality with a bump, if I was ever in reality at all. I looked down and saw I had collided with a low table, which had wrought-iron legs and a marble top, somewhat similar to an old-fashioned fishmonger's counter. On it lay the stiff, unwelcoming form of a ghastly corpse. I jumped back and looked away, convinced I had escaped from one hallucination only to fall prey to another, even less appetising one. I stole another glance at the table to make sure the body was still there; when I saw it was, I almost fainted. Not only that, but I recognised the dead man as the ubiquitous Swede whom I had left sitting in a chair at my sister's flat the previous night. His once firm flesh now looked to be as soft and spongy as boarding-house stew. To add insult to injury, a low moan was coming from under the table. I knelt down and discovered my sister crouching there, sobbing her heart out. She was wearing only a filthy, torn nightdress; her hair was unkempt, and she had no shoes or make-up on.

'How did you end up in this sinister place?' I asked, upset at the distress shown by her appearance.

'You got me into this mess,' she moaned. 'I was happy while they kept you locked up on your funny farm. Ma always said that you ...'

'Stop right there,' I cut in. 'Not everything Ma said was to be taken as gospel. It's true it would help us a lot if that had been the case, but neither reason nor subsequent experience have demonstrated she was infallible.'

'... that you would look after me when she and Pa were gone,' my sister went on, 'and as you have just said so rightly, her prophecy could not have been wider of the mark.'

'Esteemed young lady,' said the black man, 'we all suffer not so much from our faults but from the prejudices which an enfeebled, unimaginative social system forces on us. Take me, for example: I always wanted to be a poet, but racial prejudice has meant that here I am, compelled to satisfy the most basic female instincts. Isn't that so, my love?'

'Well, it would have been a real waste if you'd devoted your time to writing sonnets, sweetheart,' said Mercedes, glancing lasciviously at the bulge in his underpants.

'As the classical author put it,' lamented the black man, '"I've had a long time to consider it!" I had talent. It's too late now, but I could have been someone in the art world. Look, who am I doing now?' At this, his voice became thin and reedy and he started swaying his hips. "Oh daughter, heavens above, what is this service?" You give up? The Mayor of Zalamea! How about this one? A Frenchman, an Englishman, a German and a Spaniard are all on board a plane. No? And the joke about Franco on a scooter? And the one about Avecrem? I'm a man of many talents, but where did they get me? I was robbed of the chance to play the role of Fray Escoba in that film.'

'Come, Candida,' I said to my sister, 'let's get out of here as quickly as we can.'

I stooped under the table in order to bring her out, but as I did so, my sister scratched my face and kicked me in the solar plexus, knocking all the wind out of me.

'What did you do that for?' I managed to ask before losing consciousness.

18

THE HOUSE ON THE MOUNTAIN

When I came to, the first thing I heard was a very familiar voice saying: 'Sisters, close your eyes if you don't want to see a man's nether parts. You could use the moments of reflection to say a miserere for his poor soul.'

In a faint, croaking voice I managed to murmur: 'Inspector Flores! How did you get here?'

'Don't move,' said the equally well-known voice of Dr Sugrañes, 'or I might jab your foreskin by mistake. There's not much light in here, and my hand isn't as steady as it used to be. Did I ever tell you, Inspector, that in my youth I won a clay-pigeon shooting contest? An *amateur* one, of course,' he concluded, emphasising the word with a French accent.

I realised there was quite a crowd around me: the inspector, Dr Sugrañes, Mercedes and a gaggle of nuns, among whom I recognised the Mother Superior who had visited me at the asylum. She had her arms round the sleep-walking dentist's daughter, whose nightdress was torn in several places. I asked how they had found her.

THE HOUSE ON THE MOUNTAIN

'You were all over her under this table here, you miserable immigrant paedophile,' said Inspector Flores. 'But apparently you didn't get very far, according to the manual inspection Dr Sugrañes has just carried out.'

'You still haven't told me how you got here.'

'I followed your instructions and called them,' said Mercedes, as she pulled down my trousers so that Dr Sugrañes could give me an injection.

'What about the black man?' I asked.

'There is no black man,' the doctor replied. 'You've been fantasising, as usual.'

'I'm not crazy!' I protested.

'That's for me to decide,' said Dr Sugrañes, in the cool professional tone he employed to hide his irritation.

I felt someone wipe a wet piece of cotton wool on my backside, and then a sharp prick. A bitter taste filled my mouth, and I was momentarily blinded by a sudden flash of light. When I could see again, I noticed Inspector Flores was wiping his hands with more cotton wool, and was saying to Mercedes:

'Don't touch him if you want to avoid catching tetanus. You can open your eyes now, ladies, the carnal danger is past. You may also return to your rooms. The doctor and your humble servant here will take care of everything. When it comes to legal proceedings, I will keep you informed.'

'Will we have to testify, Inspector?' the Mother Superior wanted to know.

'That's for the prosecution to decide.'

'I'm only asking because if that's the case, we'll have to

get permission from the bishop. If they don't abolish the concordat with Rome beforehand, that is.'

The nuns filed out, taking the girl with them. Only the inspector, Dr Sugrañes, Mercedes and I remained in the crypt.

'In my fantasies I also saw a dead body,' I said to the doctor. 'I'm glad to know it was all a hallucination.'

'Unfortunately not, shitface,' said the inspector. 'You didn't invent the corpse. If you raise that sheet, you'll see it.'

He pointed towards a macabre heap on the floor. I asked him to explain.

'All in good time,' he said. 'But while we're here, let's see where this passageway leads.' He took a revolver out of his back pocket and spun it round in his hand. 'Follow me and make sure you're out of the line of fire. What with all the austerity measures the new government has brought in, I haven't had much chance to practise. I'm not sure of my aim any more. And to think I was almost chosen for the Tokyo Olympics!'

'It's always the same in our country,' said Dr Sugrañes, 'anyone with talent immediately makes others jealous. How do you feel?'

'I can walk,' I replied. 'But aren't we simply straying into another labyrinth?'

'It doesn't look like it,' said the inspector from inside the passage. 'Besides, if this is like the last one, it's a joke.'

'Why do you say that?'

'All those other tunnels led to the crypt,' Dr Sugrañes

explained. 'They must have been put there for their psychological effect: to discourage anyone who found the entrance. But whoever built them didn't want to fall into his own trap, and made sure that, as the saying goes, all roads led to Rome.'

With the inspector in the lead, we left the crypt behind and disappeared into the passageway that led off in the opposite direction to the tunnels I had got lost in. The inspector was carrying a torch whose batteries seemed on the point of giving out. Behind him came Dr Sugrañes, still brandishing his hypodermic syringe, while I brought up the rear, leaning heavily on Mercedes because I felt so weak and disheartened. We walked straight ahead for some way, but all came to a halt when we heard the inspector cursing.

'There's some steps here. I didn't see them and almost broke my neck,' he said. 'These torches they send us from Madrid are useless. Some minister's relative must be making a fortune out of them.'

We climbed the stairs and found ourselves faced by an iron door. The inspector tried to open it, but it wouldn't budge.

'If you have a bit of wire, I'll do it for you,' I offered.

Mercedes gave me a hairpin, which I straightened out to make a lock-pick. Once I had solved the problem, we all found ourselves in a huge room filled with rusting machinery covered in dust. At the far end were some metal shutters, and beside them stood a dilapidated carriage, out of which suddenly flew a flock of bats squeaking noisily. Mercedes struggled to contain a cry of horror.

'What the fuck is this?' spluttered Inspector Flores.

'From the tracks,' said Dr Sugrañes, 'I would say it's a disused funicular railway.'

'Let's see where it goes,' the inspector said. 'You there, get these shutters open.'

It took me some time and effort, but I eventually succeeded in unlocking the mechanisms and springs on the shutters, and we were able to slide them back. By the early morning light we could see the funicular's tracks disappearing up a mountainside.

'Do you think this thing works?' said the inspector, to no one in particular.

'I'll have a look,' said Dr Sugrañes. 'These days, with all the advances in medicine, we practitioners need to know a bit about mechanics.'

He began banging and hammering at the machinery. Somewhat revived by the cool morning air, I asked the inspector to give me the explanations he had promised.

'This young lady here,' he said, pointing to Mercedes, who seemed strangely hostile, 'whom I met six years ago, and who may I say has only improved since then, called me at half past two this morning and told me what you were up to. Worried you might cause more trouble, I informed Dr Sugrañes, who nobly offered to help me recapture you. Together we made our way to the school, where we explained what had happened to the nuns. They accompanied us to the crypt to make sure we did not violate holy ground. With the aid of votive candles from the chapel, we explored the labyrinth, and as the doctor has already told you, discovered that in fact it was no such thing, but a trick designed to put anyone who found their way into it off the scent. The fact that the labyrinth did not continue on the other side of the crypt may mean either that the whole thing was simply intended as a way of escape from the building, or that the money ran out halfway through the project. However that may be, we reached the crypt and found you underneath the table with the body on it, clutching a poor girl whose nightdress you had torn to pieces with your demented lunges.'

At this point we heard a shout from Dr Sugrañes:

'Glory be! I've done it!'

It was true: the funicular began to move forward, so we all jumped on board and sat on seats covered in dust and bats' poo.

'What I don't understand,' said the inspector as the car rose slowly through fragrant pine trees, 'is why you didn't tell me what you had found out, and what you intended to do. It would have saved you a lot of effort, and avoided quite a few dangers.'

'I wanted to show that I could do it myself.'

'Distrust of the forces of law and order is an endemic problem in this country,' said the inspector severely.

'It all stems from parent–child relations among the lower classes,' Dr Sugrañes opined.

I cast a sideways glance at Mercedes, who had remained silent the whole time. Her head, shoulders and even the most prominent part of her anatomy seemed to be drooping. She appeared to be showing a more than usual interest in the grey, misty city we got occasional glimpses of at our feet. As day advanced, the streetlights and the lights around the tourist monuments clicked off automatically. All that was left were the colourful adverts dotted round Plaza Catalunya. Smoke rose from a ferryboat in the port, while the stark lines of an aircraft carrier from the Sixth Fleet stood out on the horizon. I reflected sadly on how pleased my sister would have been to see all those potential clients. A sudden cry roused me from my daydreams.

'Watch out, we're going to crash!'

The funicular had reached the upper end of its trajectory, and was heading at full speed towards another pair of metal shutters. A split second before it smashed into them, we all leapt free. The car exploded in a shower of wood and iron, but pierced the shutters and continued inexorably on its way until it crashed into another engine room full of wheels, cables and other gear. Sparks began to fly, then purple flashes shot up into the air, until in a few minutes the whole thing was reduced to a pile of scrap iron.

'Now look what you've gone and done!' growled the inspector, shaking off the bits of grass and earth he had got on his Maxcali suit as he rolled down the mountainside.

'Let's see where we are,' said the ever-practical Dr Sugrañes.

We walked round what was left of the wheel-house and found ourselves in a gentle meadow with a big house in the middle of it. Standing in their nightclothes in the mansion doorway was a family who had been woken by the crash. The inspector asked them to identify themselves, which they did without a fuss. They were honest citizens who had bought the house and land ten years earlier. They knew of the funicular, but had never used it, and had no idea where it went. They offered us breakfast, and the inspector was able to call from the house for a patrol car to come and fetch us.

'It's not every trail that leads to spectacular results,' mused the inspector as he savoured his milky coffee. 'It's all part of police routine.'

The family's youngest son stared at him in open-mouthed admiration. They wanted to give me breakfast in the kitchen, but Dr Sugrañes insisted he wouldn't let me out of his sight. My presence cast something of a pall on the festive proceedings.

19

THE MYSTERY OF THE CRYPT,
SOLVED AT LAST

Once we were all crammed together in the police car and speeding down towards Barcelona, I thought the moment had come to clear up the many remaining obscure points in the chain of events I had been so much a part of.

'Of course, it was what Mercedes told me that gave me the clue to the puzzle. Until then, it had not occurred to me that the Swedish sailor and the girl's disappearance might be in some way related. Now I see it all clearly, and in order for you to do the same, I'll begin at the beginning.

'It's clear that Peraplana was, and doubtless still is, mixed up in some shady business: drugs perhaps, if not something even shadier. To discover exactly what that is, all you need do is examine his official and secret account books. Six years ago, probably at the start of his criminal activities, somebody found out what he was up to, or already knew about it, and threatened to tell the police. I wouldn't rule out the possibility of blackmail; in fact, I think that's the most likely explanation. However that may be, Peraplana or his henchmen killed that person. Peraplana was and still is a man of influence, but not to the extent of being able to escape a murder charge if the body were discovered, as was doubtless about to happen in this case. He therefore decided to conceal the crime behind another which the police would soon close the file on, thereby inadvertently burying both of them together, since the two would inevitably be linked. I think I've made that sufficiently clear, haven't I?

'At that time, Peraplana's only daughter was a boarder at a famous school situated in a mansion that had once belonged to him, which he had disposed of for financial reasons I won't go into here. The property had been built by one Vicenzo Hermafrodito Halfmann, a person of obscure origin and mysterious movements, who settled in Barcelona during the First World War. *v.h.h.* built a secret passage out of the house, disguising it as a tomb. This passage led to a funicular which connected his residence with the house on the mountain – for purposes which I would like to think were lewd, but which were probably political. Peraplana discovered the secret passage and the crypt, but the mountain house did not belong to him, and so he had no use for them. Some years later, he remembered the passage and thought it might be useful, well aware that the nuns had no idea it existed.'

'Thanks either to a depraved nun or some other subterfuge, he gave his daughter a drug, which he must have obtained from his milk factory, where I believe they use it to make their products more attractive to their customers. He brought the dead body to the crypt, then went in search of his daughter, who was sleeping obliviously all the while. His original plan was for the police to discover the stiff while they were investigating the young girl's disappearance, and, so as not to involve an innocent person in such a scandal, to drop the case. But then Mercedes got in the way, and everything became more complicated. She followed Peraplana without being seen, and saw him taking poor Isabel down to the crypt. I reckon the drug they had given Isabel soon wore off, so to keep her unconscious they had to give her ether as well. Mercedes inhaled this, and became a prey to hallucinations that were a mixture of reality and desire. It happens to all of us, with or without ether, and there's no shame in that. Despite being fuddled by the gas however, Mercedes discovered the dead body and decided, possibly as a result of secret antipathies, that it was Isabel who had murdered him. She never imagined there was anyone else in the crypt, since when she saw the mask Peraplana was wearing to protect himself from the ether, she thought it was a huge fly. The Wambas that both the murder victim and Peraplana were wearing (in those days, it was a very popular make of shoe) only served to compound her mistake. Out of affection for Isabel, Mercedes decided to take responsibility for the crime she thought her best friend had committed. She therefore accepted Peraplana's proposal to exile herself in the countryside: for his part, he wanted her out of the way, and yet did not wish to complicate matters still further with another murder.

'The plan was a success, and Peraplana came out of it safe and sound. But then, six years later, another blackmailer forced him to repeat the crime. This time however, Peraplana had learnt from experience. He made sure that the dentist's daughter disappeared (with her father's consent) before he killed his victim. It was perhaps at that moment – although this is only a guess – that he found out I was involved in the case, and thought he would not need to use the crypt after all, but could pin the murder directly on me. Correctly surmising I would get in touch with my sister, he sent the Swede to her, claiming she would pay him off. My sister didn't know what to make of the sailor's demands, but, accustomed as she is to the eccentricities of a far from select clientele, she blithely ignored them. As Peraplana had calculated, the enraged Swede came after me. He was probably an addict, so at some point Peraplana slipped him drugs containing a slow poison. The Swede came to my room to die and Peraplana, in cahoots no doubt with the one-eyed hotel porter, sent the police to catch me in flagrante. I escaped in the nick of time, but the police were in hot pursuit, so Peraplana and the one-eyed man transported the dead body to my sister's flat. When I got there, I found him dead a second time, but once again managed to escape, thanks to a corrupt police inspector. Since I was on the scene, Peraplana decided there was no point keeping the girl hidden, and so exactly as he had done with Isabel, had her brought back to her bed. When he realised I intended to investigate the crypt, he took the Swede's body there, and goodness knows what else he might have done had not the sudden, unfortunate death of his daughter wreathed his mind in clouds of grief. I then found my way down to the crypt, and fell victim to the ether they had released for that purpose, and which the lack of ventilation meant was still effective. It's quite possible it was only your timely intervention that saved me from further danger. That's all.'

This was followed by a lengthy silence, which Inspector Flores eventually broke to ask: 'So now what?'

'What do you mean, what?' I said. 'The case is solved.'

'That's easy enough to say,' said the inspector. 'But in practice ...' he left the phrase dangling in mid-air, lit a cigar, and for the first time since I had met him, addressed me as if I were someone with a brain in my head. 'I'll tell you the problems straight out. First of all, there's you. As I see it, you've only just been released from an asylum, and you're wanted for the following offences: concealing a crime, disobeying a police officer, assaulting the security forces, possessing and dealing in prohibited substances, robbery, breaking-and-entering, identity fraud, abuse of a minor, and the desecration of tombs.'

'I was only doing my duty,' I said feebly.

'Tell that to the prosecuting magistrate. Taking into account all the extenuating circumstances, you're still looking at a lengthy prison sentence. And there won't be another amnesty for forty years.'

He took several puffs on his cigar. Dr Sugrañes coughed in protest.

'As a public official,' the inspector went on, 'I am not in a position to suggest anything. However, a sensible and

THE MYSTERY OF THE CRYPT, SOLVED AT LAST

impartial observer such as Dr Sugrañes here might decide it's better to leave things as they are. What do you say, Doctor?'

'As long as I don't have to sign anything,' replied the doctor, 'that's fine by me.'

'Personally, I'm quite happy to go on with the case,' said the inspector. 'It would mean lots of overtime, which is well paid. But what about all the fuss, the paperwork, the interviews, the witness statements, all the legal procedures an affair like this implies? Isn't it worth the occasional sacrifice now and then for a quiet life? If we took the opposite view, where would it get us? The two dead men were disgusting blackmailers who got their just deserts. By the way, you ought to know that Isabel Peraplana did not die. The silly girl swallowed three aspirins, five cough sweets and a couple of suppositories, trying to commit suicide. Nothing a good laxative couldn't take care of. There was no real need to call an ambulance, but you know what people with money are like: at the first sign of a migraine they book themselves into intensive care. What would happen to the poor girl if we brought all her father's shenanigans out into the open? As for the silent but resplendent young lady here in the car with us, wouldn't she find herself at least morally guilty of murder? Think of all the scandal she would be involved in if it emerged she had been kept for six years by a criminal, whether to keep her quiet, or for other favours I prefer not to mention here? Thanks to you, this delightful young woman is free of all suspicion, and the remorse she feels for causing Isabel's death will ease now she knows her friend will soon get over it. There is nothing to stop her leaving behind for ever both a painful exile and a murky past, and to return to the exciting life of Barcelona, where she can take a degree in Humanities, become a Trotskyist, go to London for an abortion; in short, live a happy life. Are you willing to compromise such a brilliant future simply out of a desire for notoriety?'

I looked across at Mercedes, who was staring fixedly out of the car window. Since we had been stuck at a traffic light for some time now, I deduced she didn't want me to see her face.

'Promise me you'll release my sister,' I said to the inspector, 'and it's a deal.'

Flores laughed heartily.

'You always were an opportunist!' he said. 'I promise to do whatever I can. As you know, nowadays I don't have the influence I once had. It depends above all on who wins the elections.'

'Okay,' I said, realising I had no further bargaining power.

The patrol car leapt forward some fifty metres, then came to a stop once more.

'I think this is where you get off, young lady,' the inspector said to Mercedes. 'If you like bullfighting, give me a call: I've got front row seats.'

Mercedes got out without saying a word. I watched her mouth-watering melons disappear among the crowd. The inspector spoke again:

'It will be my pleasure to accompany you back to the asylum.'

He told the driver: 'Ramón, try the ring-road, and if that's no better, put the siren on.'

With a couple of skilful manoeuvres, the driver extricated us from the jam, and we were soon speeding along the street. I realised that once I had done a deal with the inspector, there was no further need for us to be stuck in traffic. Out of the window I saw the city flashing by: houses and more houses, blocks of flats and empty lots, noxious factories, walls painted with the hammer and sickle and initials I didn't understand, then dank fields and streams full of polluted water, clusters of electricity pylons and mounds of industrial waste, neighbourhoods with unlikely-looking chalets, tennis courts for hire by the hour (cheaper in the morning), hoardings announcing future dream residences, petrol stations selling pizza, plots of land for sale, 'traditional' restaurants, and a huge, half-torn Iberia advert, then sad villages and pine woods. As we sped by, I was thinking to myself that after all I had not had such a bad time; that I had solved a complicated case, even if there were several very dubious loose ends to be tied up; that I had been able to enjoy a few days of freedom; and above all, that I had met a beautiful, wonderful woman towards whom I bore no ill will, and whom I would always remember. I also thought I might be able to get the football team together again and finally this year play against the schizos from Pere Mata and, who knows, if we were lucky, even win the cup from them. And I recalled there was a new mental retard in the south

ward who seemed to be giving me the come-on, and that
the wife of a Popular Alliance candidate had promised the
asylum a colour TV if her husband won the election; that
I could at last take a shower and perhaps even have a Pepsi,
provided Dr Sugrañes was not too annoyed with me for
having got him involved in the funicular disaster; and that
just because something doesn't work out as you had hoped
doesn't mean it's the end of the world; that there would be
other opportunities to prove I really was sane, and that if
they didn't arise, I would be able to find them.